Winter Park
PUBLIC LIBRARY

Presented by

The
Rachel D. Murrah

Fiction
Endowment Book Fund

The Suicide Collectors

The Suicide Collectors

David Oppegaard

St. Martin's Press ❧ *New York*

H

Excerpt from *The Elements of Style,* 4th ed., by William Strunk Jr. and E. B. White, copyright © 2000 by Allyn & Bacon. Reprinted by permission of Pearson Education, Inc.

www.stmartins.com

Book design by Michael Collica

LIBRARY OF CONGRESS CATALOGING-IN-PUBLICATION DATA

Oppegaard, David.
   The suicide collectors / David Oppegaard.—1st ed.
      p. cm.
   ISBN-13: 978-0-312-38110-3
   ISBN-10: 0-312-38110-7
   1. Mass suicide—Fiction.   2. Survival skills—Fiction.
I. Title.
   PS3615.P63S85   2008
   813'.6—dc22   2008025782

First Edition: December 2008

1   3   5   7   9   10   8   6   4   2

For my mother, Kayc Kline

Acknowledgments

The author would like to thank his friends and family for all their love, support, good humor, and red wine. He would also like to thank his agent, Jonathan Lyons, for digging in his heels and championing the author's work. Thank you to his editor, Michael Homler, production editor Kenneth J. Silver, and the entire hardworking St. Martin's Press crew. The deepest of thanks to his generous teachers and earliest readers: Thomas Hagen, Jim Heynen, Charles Taliaferro, Mary F. Rockcastle, Sheila O'Connor, Kelly Coyle, Lawrence Sutin, and Deborah Keenan.

Special thanks to Betty Davis, Sarah Morse, Ben Jacobson, Mike Mensink, Nathan Jorgenson, and Geoff Herbach.

A swimmer in distress cries, "I shall drown; no one will save me!" A suicide puts it the other way: "I will drown; no one shall save me!" In relaxed speech, however, the words *shall* and *will* are seldom used precisely; our ear guides us or fails to guide us, as the case may be, and we are quite likely to drown when we want to survive and survive when we want to drown.

      —Strunk and White, *The Elements of Style*, 4th ed.

PART ONE

Swampland

1

The path home was overrun with weeds and hanging vines. Norman hiked through the mess as best he could, slapping the mosquitoes against his neck as he tried to keep his fishing pole from tangling in the park's tall grass. He kept his shoulders hunched, ducking the low branches, until he'd plowed his way through the dense overgrowth and back onto a paved street.

Though the sun was out now, it had rained for days and the entire town was covered in a furry coat of moss. Green thrived on tree trunks, sidewalks, street signs, rocks, automobiles, flagpoles. Even the abandoned houses around Norman had taken on a greenish hue, their wooden walls decaying like the skin of a gangrenous sailor. A pale green lizard slid out from beneath a sunken car, shook its head, and looked up at Norman. It stuck its forked tongue into the air, as if trying to taste human on the wind. Norman considered catching the lizard, maybe frying it with bananas and salt, but decided against it. He was already late for lunch. Jordan, his wife, liked to eat at exact, predetermined times. She claimed the routine gave her a better sense of day and night, of the weeks and months passing.

Norman waved his fishing pole at the lizard and continued walking. Just under six feet tall, Norman had an average build, a Floridian's brown tan, and hair so dark it was almost black. He didn't examine the rows of empty, sagging homes around him, preferring to keep his eyes fixed on the cracked street. After five years Norman was tired of tracking the town's slow crumble, of noting which roof had collapsed, what fence had fallen over, whose rusted swing set had fallen apart. If people wanted to leave their lives behind, that was their business, not his. He was still only thirty-four. He had his own life to attend to, his own house to guard.

Norman turned down another quiet street, weaving around the occasional rusting car. His house was up ahead. Pops, their sole remaining neighbor in a town that had once had a population of over four thousand, sat on his front porch, muttering as he tinkered with a corroded electric generator. A bald, strong old man with grease-stained fingernails, Pops wore dark sunglasses and the faded denim overalls of an auto mechanic. He glanced up as Norman's shadow fell across his porch and sat back from the generator. He wiped sweat off his forehead with the back of one large hand and nodded.

"Afternoon, Norman."

"Afternoon, Pops. Fix anything today?"

Pops pushed his wraparound sunglasses up his nose and

smacked his thick lips. "If I can get it running again, this old generator might be useful. We could always use a few more around here."

"No kidding. Well, good luck."

Long, wet grass squelched beneath Norman as he walked across his lawn. He took off his muddy boots, set his fishing pole down on the porch, and went inside. The living room was dim, its curtains drawn. This was unusual. Jordan loved a bright house and always woke a little after dawn. The curtains should have been open for hours already, allowing sunlight to pour into their living room and feed his wife's thriving collection of potted plants.

"Jordan?"

Norman slid across the hardwood floor in his socks. He sniffed the air for a scent of lunch but caught nothing. The kitchen was dark. Norman opened the back door and peeked into the yard, scanning their vegetable garden for his wife. Not there, either. He headed upstairs. The stairway, hallway, and bathroom were all dark. He turned the knob of their bedroom door and entered the perfumed silence of their room. Here darkness had settled over everything like dust, piling up on their dressers, their nightstands, in each corner of the room. Norman drew open the curtains to let the sunlight in. A lumpy shape lay in the center of their queen bed, hidden by a white comforter.

"Morning, hon," Norman said. "It's a beautiful day out there. Blue skies, but not too hot yet. We should tackle the garden."

Sunlight revealed only the top of his wife's head, a tangled mass of blond hair peeking out from under a blanket. The bed creaked under Norman's weight as he pounced. "Time to get up, sleepy." Norman felt through the blanket, found a shoulder, and gave it a shake. His wife didn't move at the encouragement.

"Come on, sweetheart. We'll make some lunch."

Jordan failed to respond to more shaking so Norman pulled the blanket back. Her body was curved inward in the fetal position. Her pajama tank top was bunched between her breasts, and as Norman watched her chest, he felt a chill spread through him.

She wasn't breathing.

"Honey?"

Norman put two fingers to her throat. No pulse, and her skin was clammy. On their nightstand an empty bottle of sleeping pills was tipped over on its side.

A moan slid out from the back of Norman's throat. He took off all his clothes. He climbed back into the bed and wrapped himself around his wife's body. He made sure the blankets covered her feet, which were always cold, and nuzzled the back of her neck with his nose. He exhaled batches of hot air, filling the room with as much warmth as he could.

An hour later Norman made noise in his garage, knocking over coffee cans and sweeping aside tools. He opened drawers and cabinets. He riffled through bins, trunks, buckets, and

cardboard boxes. Amazing how much junk he had accumu-
lated over the years, like an overzealous squirrel storing up
more acorns than it could ever possibly eat. Had he really
thought all this crap could prevent anything? What good
were electrical tape, handsaws, road flares, and industrial-
size space heaters versus an empty phonebook?

Norman kicked a cinder block and winced as it toppled
over. He cursed and returned to his search. The Collectors
would soon be here. They'd come in numbers, silent and
dark-robed, and glide up his front-porch steps like ghosts.
They would open his door without knocking. They would
fan out, find what they wanted, and take it without a word.

He found his shotgun in a bottom drawer in the dimmest
corner of the garage. It smelled like oil and sulfur, but he
liked its weight in his hands. A box of unused shells sat in the
drawer, behind a stack of old magazines. Their neon-red cas-
ings glowed despite the dim light. Norman slowly pushed
five shells into the shotgun, as if feeding it large medicinal
pills, and racked the first shell into the shotgun's chamber.
Was that creaking coming from the house?

Norman disengaged the shotgun's safety as he walked
back inside. He flipped on every light in every room but left
the curtains drawn. He went upstairs, flipping on more
lights, and checked on his wife. She was still lying on her
side, covered by the white comforter. Below their bedroom
window, in the backyard, a rabbit nibbled on rhubarb leaves
in the garden. No signs of intruders, no Collectors wading
through the swamp that edged their yard. Norman closed

the curtains and made sure the windows were locked. He
went back downstairs. He poured himself a glass of whiskey
and went out to the front porch. He sat down in his favorite
rocking chair, set the shotgun across his lap, and started to
drink.

Pops was no longer out working on his own front porch.
The old man was probably inside, avoiding the worst of
the day's heat. Mosquitoes swarmed Norman's face as they
searched for a vulnerable place to land. He swatted them
away and peered down both ends of the street. Which way
would the Collectors come from? The surrounding streets
and highways were pretty much underwater, bogged out by
swamps reclaiming their turf. It would be difficult to drive
any sort of vehicle through—

What was that noise?

Norman cocked his head. Where had he heard that sound
before? As if someone were beating the sky with a paddle, the
way you aired out large, dusty rugs. The noise was above
town now—*whump whump whump*—and its fierce mechanical sound caused Norman to down the rest of his whiskey in
one gulp.

Pops had come back out. "I know that sound," the old
man shouted from his porch. "What's happened, Norman?
Where's your wife?" Pops' eyes fell on the shotgun in Norman's hands. He ran a hand over his bald head and cleared
his throat.

"Don't, son. I know she meant the world to you, but don't
do it."

Norman checked to make certain the shotgun's safety was still off.

"Sorry, Pops."

Norman ran inside his house. The mechanical roar was now directly overhead, as if an enraged dragon had perched on their roof. Norman sprinted to the second floor. He kicked open the bedroom door, the shotgun's stock pressed tight against the crook of his shoulder. Three Collectors were already bent over his wife's bed, their dark robes flapping as a gale poured in through the room's broken window. The word *helicopter* finally came to Norman. He fired into the ceiling, scattering plaster everywhere.

The figures turned toward him. Their faces were pale and smooth, like polished skulls. Hardly human at all. Norman racked another shell into the shotgun's chamber, but he kept the gun pointed at the ceiling.

"Don't touch her, goddamn it."

The largest of the Collectors, a big man with broad shoulders and a square face, turned his back to Norman and lifted Jordan into his arms. The other two Collectors, a slender man and a woman with gray eyes, parted as the big man walked toward the window and the waiting helicopter outside. Norman lowered the shotgun's barrel and drew a bead on the big man's back. The Collector continued to the window, carrying Jordan's limp body easily, as if death had already hollowed her out. Norman clenched his teeth and squeezed the shotgun's trigger.

A deafening roar and the big man's head disappeared. The Collector's body took one more quivering step, paused, and slumped forward onto the floor, dropping its burden. Jordan's body rolled over, onto its back. The other Collectors looked from their headless colleague to Norman. Blood and pulped flesh had splattered onto their faces, flecks of white bone stood out against the dark cloth of their robes. Norman nodded toward the headless body.

"Take him instead."

The Collectors converged on the fresh corpse. One grabbed it by the hands and another grabbed it by the feet. They took it to the window, secured it in a sling made out of nylon webbing, and pushed the corpse outside with the ease of long practice. Attached to the helicopter by a thick winch cable, the harnessed body hung swinging in mid-air, like a pendulum, and first one and then the other Collector leaped out the window after it, clinging to its bulk as it lifted higher into the air.

Norman sank to his knees. He set the shotgun on the floor and bowed his head. He waited for a spray of bullets, for machine-gun retribution, but the helicopter simply rose above the house and flew away. The bedroom returned to its former quiet. Norman saw that his wife's eyes were open and staring through him. He rolled them shut. A low, steady hum filled his mind, like a summons to something still far off, and when Norman covered his ears, the sound just grew louder.

2

Norman and Pops buried Jordan in the dark. They worked rapidly by the light of a golf cart's halogen headlights, shoveling wet clumps of dirt with as little wasted movement as possible, their breathing regular and loud. The day's heat lingered and it was still too warm for work like this, but Norman didn't want his wife's corpse exposed to further trouble. The Collectors had left, dragging one of their dead with them, but that didn't mean the spooky bastards wouldn't come back and try again. For nearly five years Norman and Pops had peacefully opposed the Collectors from their small Florida town, burying suicides before the Collectors could arrive on-site. They hadn't saved every corpse from being dragged away (so many of the suicides went in the middle of the night, with sleeping pills or some other poison), but they had saved enough to realize the Collectors wouldn't give up until the body was buried six feet deep.

When the hole was deep enough, they lowered Jordan's body into it. She was wrapped in a white cotton bedsheet, the nicest one Norman could find in their linen closet. They shoveled dirt into the hole without pause until the grave was filled. Norman stepped back and rested his chin on the handle of his shovel. The night air smelled like acrid swamp gas and blooming orchids. Pops shoveled more dirt until a mound rose above the grave. Norman considered saying a poem, something eulogy-like, but couldn't think of anything. The night-shift mosquitoes had found him. They crawled over his forearms, neck, and face, prodding his skin for blood.

Pops took their shovels and tossed them into the back of the golf cart. The cart had been modified over the years as Pops, a natural mechanic, tinkered with it almost daily. The cart now had oversize wheels, roll bars, seat belts, and an engine twice as powerful as the factory original (the cart could break fifty on a flat stretch of road). Pops sat down in the driver's seat and rubbed his hands together. "Well," he said, "let's go get drunk."

Norman got into the cart and buckled his seat belt. Pops drove fast through the deserted streets, weaving between the stalled vehicles, cars and trucks whose locations he had memorized long ago and regarded with as much interest as the passing palm trees. Bugs smashed against the cart's grill as they rounded a sharp turn. A large chunk of darkness appeared ahead, squatting in the middle of the road. Pops gunned the golf cart's engine and headed straight for it. Norman pushed his foot to the passenger-side floor, searching for a brake pedal that wasn't there.

"It's too big, Pops. You'll flip us."

"Hmmm. Well, we better find out for sure."

Norman swore as the cart slammed into the chunk of darkness. Its front end bucked upward as its wheels rose from the earth. Stars blurred into view. A bug flew into Norman's open mouth and stuck against the back of his throat. They hung in the sky for what seemed like a long time, weightless except for a slight downward tug, then the cart crashed back onto the road. The hard landing caused Norman's body to pitch forward against his seat belt, and he swallowed the bug.

Pops fought the steering wheel for control of the cart. They skidded off the road, up a curb, and back into the street. Pops pounded Norman on the back as he tried to cough up the bug. "She can really fly, can't she? One fallen branch, and we're off like the Wright brothers."

They passed more dead vehicles and thriving palm trees in the warm darkness. Norman sat back, enjoying the fragrant breeze that blew across his face. Pops pulled into the parking lot of an old strip mall and stopped in front of a faded awning that read LIQUOR IS QUICKER. The cart's headlights illuminated the front end of the store's interior, revealing several dazzling patches of broken glass. Pops elbowed Norman in the ribs.

"What should we get tonight, son? I feel like a little Jack Daniel's myself. Actually, I feel like a lot of it."

Norman unbuckled his seat belt. "Hell. I'll drink lighter fluid, for all I care."

Norman and Pops headed for the hard liquor, kicking away the empty cardboard boxes that littered the store's linoleum floor. Most of the stock had gone bad years ago, and the store smelled like old hops and vinegar. "Ah, my good friend," Pops said, picking up a bottle of whiskey and examining its label. Norman grabbed a bottle of clear and a bottle of golden for himself, not bothering to read their labels. He turned to leave, but something in the aisle was crawling toward them.

"Pops," Norman whispered. The crawling thing was log-shaped. Big.

"Yeah?"

"Look."

The old man turned and whistled. "Well, I'll be damned. Alligator."

Norman and Pops stepped backward. The alligator slid forward and cracked its mouth open, revealing an extensive, shadowy nest of teeth.

And what was that smell?

Raw meat?

"This is how folks lose legs," Pops whispered. "You know that? This is how people lose legs."

"Yes. I know that."

"We should run."

Norman glanced back at the door without actually turning his head. The front door appeared very far away at the moment.

"Okay. You first."

"Why me?"

"You're old and you're slow. You need the head start worse. You run, and I'll chuck this bottle at him."

"But that's the last tequila in town."

"Run, you lush."

Pops ran and the alligator leaped forward. Norman hurled the tequila bottle as hard as he could. The bottle hit the patch of linoleum in front of the alligator's snout, missing it totally, but the crash did make it flinch and draw back. Norman sprinted after the old man. He didn't look back as he ran (he needed to concentrate on hurdling all the empty cardboard boxes), but Norman could hear the gator snapping its jaws as it slithered across the floor after them.

Norman reached the front door first despite Pops' head start. The old man was still huffing down the bargain-wine aisle, the alligator snapping at his ankles as he pumped his thick arms. Norman stepped outside the store and held the front door open. The old man dove through the doorway headfirst, and Norman slammed the door shut after him. The gator's snout smashed into the door, sending a tiny ripple of cracks across the reinforced glass. Norman leaned back against the door, sucking air. Pops wheezed laughter from the sidewalk.

"It's official, Norman," the old man said, holding up his

intact bottle of whiskey in the golf cart's headlights. "It's still good to be alive."

Pops' dining room smelled like engine oil and burned fish. They drank at Pops' well-scarred dinner table, surrounded by a lifetime of mechanical aptitude. Around them sat a disassembled motorcycle engine, three retired video monitors, and several industrial batteries of various sizes. Aluminum shelves held an assortment of cut wood, tin cans full of nails, and buckets full of cannibalized electronics. Socket sets, socket wrenches. Bolts. Clamps. Needle-nose pliers. Electrical tape. Box cutters. Handsaws. Depleted propane tanks. Brake pads. Tires, flat and otherwise. Stacks of faded yellow repair manuals. Piles of old hot-rod magazines. An assortment of maps and books, newspapers and warranty cards now only useful as scrap paper. Coffee-stained notepads, totally covered with roughly sketched diagrams of devices Norman didn't recognize.

They hadn't spoken since they'd returned from the liquor store. Norman kept seeing the Collector's head as it vaporized. He concentrated on downing drink after drink.

"I still can't believe you did that," Pops said, guessing Norman's thoughts. "You shot one. You shot a dark robe."

Norman looked up from his drink to find the old man staring at him, his magnified eyes bloodshot behind his thick spectacle lenses. Norman ran his fingers through his hair. He could still feel a flat spot where Jordan's hand had slipped last week, cutting too much.

"I didn't think I'd have to kill anyone. Thought I could scare them away."

Pops drummed the table with his grease-stained fingers. He filled Norman's tumbler with more whiskey and pushed it forward. "I don't think you should lose any sleep over what you did today, Norman. They've had it coming for a long time. Hell, I wish I'd thought of fighting back when my Helen died. I was too sad, I suppose. Nothing mattered anymore, so why do anything? Well, you know the old story." Pops took a sip of whiskey and grinned. "But you, Norman. You still have some steel in you, my son."

Norman took a drink, already looking forward to his next.

"Killing someone isn't so hard," he said. "I aimed for the guy's head. I pulled the trigger. In the old days, I'd be in jail right now. I'd be calling a lawyer."

Pops nodded. "Maybe so, but the Despair's changed a lot of things, son. Different times, different rules. All I can tell you is a lot of good people are gone now, and all we can do is keep rolling with the punches until whatever it is that's been eating at us goes away. We don't want to give the Collectors two more trophies, do we?"

"No."

"*Hell* no, you mean. *Hell* no."

Norman cupped his drink and closed his eyes. They'd

gotten married out of college, only twenty-two. It had been an outdoor, autumn wedding up in Vermont, where Jordan had grown up. Crackling gold, scarlet, and rust-colored leaves had been scattered underfoot, fluttering down from the old trees around them. Jordan had worn a simple white dress that dipped in front, revealing a plump, promising hint of cleavage. Her cheeks had been pink with the autumn chill, her blond hair down around her shoulders, and she smiled when he slid the ring on her finger, as if that cold bit of metal had been the best thing she'd ever felt.

Norman opened his eyes. "I should have been there, you know. When she woke up this morning."

Pops rubbed his whiskered jaw and crossed his arms across his chest. "Jordan made up her mind, just like the rest of them, and no way were you going to change it. She loved you, sure as hell, but when someone gets to truly believing, I mean truly *believing*, the best choice for them is death, your arguments don't hold much water anymore. Damn, Norman, you know that as well as anyone. We've tried to argue this whole town into staying alive, and you've seen where it's gotten us. That said, I propose a toast."

"A toast?"

Pops held up his drink and waited until Norman raised his.

"To dear sweet Jordan," the old man toasted. "May her soul now rest in heaven, beyond the worries and pain of this world. Beyond the daily struggles of us, the Last Ten Percent."

"Amen, Pops."

Norman tossed back the rest of his drink. He slammed the empty tumbler down on the table, now drunk enough he could feel his teeth vibrating in his jaw. He stood up.

"Okay. I'm going home now."

Pops set his drink down. "You sure you want to sleep there tonight?"

"No. But I'm going to, anyway. It's still my house, god-damn it, and if the Collectors want to see me, they'll know where to find me, won't they?"

Pops laughed and pushed his chair back from the table.

"Okay, tough guy. Let me see you to the door."

Norman returned to his empty house. He weaved through the living room and swayed upstairs without turning on a light. Outside their bedroom he took a deep breath. He opened the door, found the light switch, and flicked it on. It was like stumbling onto an abandoned horror-movie set. Blood and flesh pulp stained the room's walls and carpet. It stank like shit and drying blood, with a tangy hint of his wife's rose-water perfume on top. Norman darted into the room and grabbed piles of his clothes and dropped them back out in the hallway. He also snatched up a few pictures, her jewelry box, and the shotgun. Then Norman went into the bathroom, dropped to his knees, and vomited into the toilet. When his stomach was empty, he went out to his garage and gathered his hammer, a box of aluminum nails, and five two-by-fours. He returned to the upstairs hallway and closed the bedroom door. He worked quickly and, despite his drunkenness, missed only the occasional nail head, the sound of his hammering loud and firm in the otherwise calm night.

When Norman finished hammering, their bedroom of ten years had been transformed into a sealed murder scene. Into a dim, forgotten place for dust to gather. A tomb. Nothing could get in, and hopefully nothing could get out, either.

3

The next morning Norman woke up on his living room couch, the house already simmering with damp heat. An empty bottle of whiskey lay on his stomach like a sleeping cat. The room was so dazzling with morning sunlight everything took on a haloed blur. "Sunglasses," Norman croaked. "Sunglasses?"

Norman's throat felt coated with sawdust. He needed water, aspirin, and some damned sunglasses.

"Jordan. Jordan. Sunglasses, please?"

Nobody answered. The house remained still. Norman rubbed his eyes and remembered his wife was dead now. He dropped the empty bottle on the floor and sat up. The ground wavered as he staggered to the kitchen and drank a quart of water while standing over the sink (five years without municipal workers, yet they still had passable running water. A damn utilities miracle). The kitchen, so long the treasured domain of his wife, already seemed to know that its true owner had abandoned it. Houses could be like that. Norman had entered dozens of ownerless homes since the beginning of the Despair, and they all gave off a similar shell-shocked vibe. No longer cared for by their human tenants, even the sturdiest homes were in danger of imploding at any moment, of cracking from the inside out and sinking into the earth. You could almost see each single particle of dust settle onto the floors and walls, one by one, happily adding to the silent pressure.

Norman filled a thermos with more water, grabbed his sunglasses, and headed outside. No clouds or wind. The Florida sun hung overhead like a bright yellow grow lamp and the town's vegetation basked in it, chlorophyll-stoned leaves unfurled. Norman wiped sweat off his forehead as he headed toward the Swamp Links golf course, about a half mile outside town.

On the way he passed homes, apartment buildings, storefronts, gift shops, luxury condos. Each building was infested with chattering insects, covered in tangled vines, and pocked with broken windows. As he passed each dilapidated structure, Norman half-expected something nasty to step out from within the ruins and come howling for him. Collector or alligator, vampire or ghoul, nothing would really surprise him. The town was haunted now. Had been for years, actually.

By the time Norman arrived at Swamp Links sweat dripped constantly into his eyes and he had to dry his forehead every few minutes with the handkerchief in his pocket. The golf course's lodge, a big wooden, faux-log-cabin-type thing, echoed with the croaking of bullfrogs, and Norman passed it without pause. He went into the garage tucked behind the lodge, started up one of the riding mowers, and drove it out to the first hole. The course's grass, lush and always on the rise, had grown six inches since his last visit. Norman smiled as he engaged the mower's blades, enjoying how the machine rumbled to life beneath him. It was nice to be around a noisy engine, to remind the insects that humans were still boss and to send the snakes winding back into the denser brush.

Norman drove the mower in swooping arcs, methodically covering the distance between the course boundaries. Originally he had trimmed the course so he could keep playing golf after the groundskeeper drowned himself in a nearby lake, but over the years Norman had ceased playing and now only mowed it to keep weeds from totally overtaking the course. He also liked to think of himself as the sole remaining proprietor of a pristine, functioning golf course in North America. Jordan had enjoyed gardening, Pops liked to rebuild old machines, but Norman prided himself in maintaining a far more useless luxury. In the old days he hadn't been able to afford a membership to the exclusive Swamp Links. Now he owned, ran, and played the course whenever the hell he wanted.

Norman stared out at the green land beyond the mower. About a year ago he'd been out mowing like this when a stranger had stepped out of the trees and waved hello. The stranger's sudden appearance hadn't been that surprising, really. They'd gotten the occasional drifter since the early days of the Despair, most of them wide-eyed and prophetic, but this drifter had spoken in a calm voice and complete sentences. He claimed to have traveled all the way across America in an effort to spread word of hope. Of a possible cure.

The drifter claimed that a Seattle scientist named Dr. Briggs was working on a cure at that very moment. Apparently this scientist was leading a resistance of sorts, a group of individuals hell-bent on remaining alive and healthy until the Despair was fully neutralized. When Norman had heard all this, the first words that had popped into his head had been *hippie cult commune,* and when the drifter had asked him, eyes gleaming, if Norman would like to return to Seattle and share in the effort, Norman had shaken the man's hand and sent him packing with a smile. Seattle, even if it was as well populated as the drifter claimed, appeared no closer than the watery mirage a thirsting man sees as he crawls across the desert.

A brown shape appeared in the grass ahead. Norman blinked out of his reverie, but not fast enough. He ran over the shape, and with a screech the mower's blades stopped and its engine stalled. Norman cursed, put the mower in park, and turned off the engine. He jumped to the ground and lay with his belly against the grass and peered under the mower. The nearest blade was crammed with a fur-covered skull, its round eyes long eaten out by bugs. Red and blue guts dripped from the mower's underside like ghoulish streamers, and Norman cursed again. He'd run over a rabbit.

A rabbit that had chosen the middle of Hole 3 to lie down and die. Christ. The smell was atrocious, and he'd have to spend an entire day unwrapping its mutilated body from the cutting blades. A freshly living rabbit would have been one thing, but this rabbit had been dead at least a week, its body exposed to the rain, baked by the sun, and finally overrun by some enthusiastic maggots.

Norman stood up. He peered into the sky and considered the dead rabbit some more, thinking about what a thing like this might mean. Then he left the bloodied, stinking mower where it was and went home.

He found Pops next door, napping in a hammock the old man had strung up between two lofty palm trees. A straw hat covered his face and a glass of water rested on the ground beside him. A water bug had landed inside the glass. It skimmed across the water's surface in speedy, zigzag motions. Norman hesitated on the driveway that separated their backyards, wondering if he should wait and let Pops rest. If the old man was anywhere near as hungover as Norman, he was much better off asleep than awake. Yet, as Norman was about to go inside, the old man grumbled beneath his hat. Norman went over to the hammock.

"You say something, Pops?"

The old man snorted and wheezed, barrel chest rising. "No, dear," Pops moaned from beneath his hat. "Please. Don't."

Norman bit his lip.

"Darling, don't. Things will come around again. They always do."

Norman bowed his head. He'd thought Pops was better. It had been five years since Helen had jumped from the town's water tower, and Pops didn't talk about it much anymore. He seemed to have moved on—

Pops shouted something, sat up too fast, and tipped out of his hammock. He landed on his knees in the grass, as if about to pray, and stared up at Norman without recognition. The old man's eyes were a wet, milky blue.

"Hey," Norman said, raising his hands. "Hey, Pops, it's alright."

"No!"

"It's okay, Pops. It's okay."

Norman grabbed the old man by the shoulders and shook him gently. Pops blinked and licked his lips.

"You're alright, Pops. You had a bad dream."

Norman pulled Pops to his feet and slapped the grass off the old man's knees. Pops pulled his sunglasses out of his coveralls and put them on with a trembling hand. "Christ," he spat.

"Bad one?"

"Worse than most."

"That shit will happen on occasion."

"Well, I wish it would happen to someone else."

"Don't we all."

Pops crossed his arms over his chest. Norman watched the

muscles in the old man's tanned forearms twitch with the gesture. Pops was still a strong man at sixty-eight. A lifetime of working on engines, homes, cars, and all his other projects had left him with a deep, lasting strength.

"Pops, I think we need to discuss recent events."

"Town meeting?"

"Town meeting."

"Alright then. What time you want me to come over?"

Norman wiped the sweat off his forehead. "Well, I'd like to take a bath first. How about in an hour?"

"One hour it is, then. I'll bring the whiskey."

"Sounds good to me."

Norman returned to his empty house and took a bath. As he sat in the steaming water, he avoided looking at the clothes piled in a corner on the bathroom floor. Jordan's clothes. His wife had culled an extensive wardrobe from the defunct stores downtown, gathering nearly every stitch of fabric in the area that was remotely her size. Her clothes were still draped upon every bookshelf, chair, and countertop on the house's second floor. Housekeeping had never been a strong point for either of them, and since the Despair they had gotten increasingly lax at picking up (the self-imposed death of almost everyone in the world put little things such as dirty T-shirts and bras in perspective). With the luxury of so many clothes at their disposal, they had fallen into the routine of doing laundry only one day a year.

Laundry Day was a big production: they would fill the bathtub with boiling water and laundry detergent, Jordan stirring the clothes with a broom handle while Norman beat them with an aluminum baseball bat. They washed dozens of laundry baskets filled with clothes, towels, sheets, blankets, and washcloths. When each basket was filled with wet, clean clothes, they took it outside to hang its contents on makeshift laundry lines, nylon cables Norman had stretched throughout the neighborhood's abandoned backyards. They spent the entire day washing clothes, laughing and drinking watered-down Scotch, and when each Laundry Day ended, they invariably found themselves on the bathroom floor, Jordan's soft body slipping against his as steam filled their house like a misty, reassuring blanket.

Norman sank into the bathtub. He allowed the warm water to rise above his head and swallow him. He ignored the tightness in his chest, the tugging he had struggled with for so many years.

After his bath Norman dressed and went downstairs. Pops sat in the living room in Norman's favorite leather recliner. His bony feet were up as he sipped water.

"Why don't you make yourself comfortable, Pops."

"Thank you, I will."

"You hungry?"

"I could eat."

Norman went into the kitchen and took two cod fillets out

of the freezer. He put a pot of water on the electric stove and turned the burner on. He got a few potatoes out of the refrigerator, sat down at the kitchen table, and started to peel. He liked the cool, rough texture of the potatoes. Jordan had grown these potatoes. She had planted, weeded, and dug up these potatoes with her own hands, in their own backyard.

Pops stepped into the kitchen.

"Can I help?"

"Nope. Have a seat and fix yourself a drink. I've got this one."

"Thanks much."

Pops sat down at the kitchen table. Norman continued peeling the garden potatoes, his back turned to the old man as he worked.

"I've been thinking, Pops. You still think that plane of yours will fly?"

"Oh, she'll fly, alright. I've fixed her up nice. Where you thinking of flying to?"

"Seattle."

Pops whistled and drummed his hands on the table. "Seattle's a long ways off."

"I know that."

"A plane's no guarantee we'd get there in one piece. Even the sky ain't safe traveling anymore. Plenty of crazies still left."

"I know that, too."

"Well."

For a few minutes the only sound in the kitchen was the

light, metallic rasp of the peeler against the potato skins. When Norman glanced at Pops, the old man was staring at his own feet, his hands clasped and resting in his lap.

"You remember what that drifter told me, don't you?" Norman said. "Twenty thousand people. Maybe more than that. A real city, Pops. Wouldn't you like to live in a real city again? Talk to people you haven't known forever?"

"Sounded like a hippie commune, didn't it?"

"It did at that time, I'll give you that. But he also said they're working on a cure. A cure for the Despair."

Pops chortled. "What? You actually believe that hogwash now? You really think they can find some sort of pill or something? After all the scientists in the world failed? Couldn't even slow it down?"

"I'd like to think so. Sure. Why not?"

"Because it's all foolishness, that's why. A pot of gold at the end of the rainbow. A bunch of hippie nonsense."

"You really think that?"

"Yes, I do."

Norman set the potatoes aside and picked his teeth with the peeler. He wondered how long it would take his teeth to rot without regular dental checkups, what it would be like to gum his food before he was sixty. One of the worst inconveniences of the fall of civilization had to be a lack of qualified doctors.

"Didn't you tell me yesterday the rules have changed? No more hippies, Pops. Just people trying to survive. People like us."

Pops shifted in his chair. "Norman, he could have been lying about the whole thing. Seattle could be totally deserted, for all we know."

"Sure. Maybe it is. But what do we have to lose anymore? We could stay here, but what's left to stay for? At least in Seattle there'll be other people. We could help them rebuild the city. I'd sure like a crack at doing something useful before I die."

"I've lived here all my life, Norman. Thought I'd die here, too."

"Enough people have died here, Pops. You can feel that as much as I can."

Pops sighed and tapped his thumbs together. "Would be interesting to see how *Jenny* flies on a longer trip."

"Sure it would be."

"And it wouldn't hurt to put some space between us and the Collectors. Never know if they're going to come back and settle the score, do we?"

"Right," Norman said, drumming his stomach as he imagined liftoff, punching through clouds. "Let's hit the road while we still can."

Pops sat forward, hands on knees. "We most likely won't be coming back, you know. What we're looking at here is a one-way trip."

"That's fine with me, Pops. Just fine."

The old man leaned back again in his chair. His milky eyes stared without focus on the space in front of him. It was that familiar zoned-out look he got when he worked on especially difficult mechanical problems. Norman dropped the peeled potatoes in the boiling water and watched them bob up and down. Bugs droned outside the kitchen windows. After he ran some water over the cod fillets, they felt slightly thawed, almost ready for the pan.

4

Norman woke from a nightmare already on his feet, shouting nonsense into the guest-room closet. His mouth was dry, and his throat ached. How long had he been shouting? How loud?

Outside, the night sky had begun to lighten. Norman's hands trembled as he dressed. He pulled out a duffel bag from the closet and began roaming the house. He grabbed photo albums and stuffed them into the bag. He grabbed her jewelry box, hair dryer, and toothbrush. Downstairs he searched her bookshelf, pulling off her favorite volumes of poetry, fiction, and nonfiction. He found a bad watercolor painting she had done and rolled this up as well, stuffing it into the bag with the other things. He also nabbed the teddy bear from Jordan's childhood, her favorite throw pillow, and the yellowed literary journal where she'd once gotten a poem published.

After he'd stuffed it full of her things, Norman lifted the

bag off the floor, felt its heft, and dumped it out onto the floor and started over. This time he packed his lucky flannel shirt, a flashlight, a can opener, seven days' worth of clean clothes, a utility knife, duct tape, matches, a poncho, nylon rope, and some bug spray. He also packed three candles, a small set of camping pots, a plate, a fork, a spoon, and a small thermal blanket. He put on his hiking boots, but ignored the shotgun.

Norman zipped his bag shut and surveyed his house one last time. He went upstairs first, locking windows and drawing the curtains. Each room looked as if it had already gone to sleep. Dust would gather in each of them, slowly settle on windowsills, desks, chairs, tables, and computers. Soon rain and insects would follow. Termites. Fat, voracious termites would feast on all the walls, floorboards, and structural beams, undermining everything. Five years from now their house would look like any other on their silent street, its roof also sagging with moss as their front porch collapsed under its own weight. There would be no evidence that he and Jordan had made it longer than most, that they had endured the brunt of the Despair only to burn out years later. Soon the entire town would again be swamp.

Norman turned all the lights off and unplugged the electrical appliances. He brought Jordan's collection of potted plants out into the backyard and set them out. He turned off the electrical generator Pops had hooked up to their home, surveyed their garden one final time, and went back inside. In the kitchen he washed the few dirty dishes in the sink and put them back into the cupboard. In the living room he placed sheets over their furniture. He breathed in the dusty living room air, picked up his duffel bag, and headed for the door.

The early morning sky was cloudy. Pops stood in their shared driveway loading a suitcase into the cargo hold of his souped-up golf cart. "Morning," Pops said, dropping his suitcase into the cart's wire basket. He took Norman's duffel bag from him. "Lock your house up?"

Norman looked back at his house. "Yeah, but I don't know why. Left the key under the welcome mat."

"Me, too. Feels strange to be leaving after all we've been through here, doesn't it? It's like we've put the entire town to bed, read it a bedtime story, and now it's time to close the door and let it sleep."

Norman stretched his arms and yawned. "Well. Might as well get on with it, then."

Pops set Norman's duffel bag on top of his own suitcase and they settled into the golf cart. They rolled quietly down the driveway and into town. The cart's electric engine was whisper quiet as they drove beneath an arch of curling palm trees. You could hear a few groggy birds call to each other, but their calls were subdued, listless. Several iguanas lay in the road, unmoving as Pops did his best to steer around them. Norman could feel his shirt clinging to his back already, caught in the sweaty press of his back and the golf cart's polyester seat. Only a slight wind today, smelling like a mixture of sulfur, oranges, and maybe a distant house fire.

"It's been a while since I've driven so early in the morning," Pops said. "I like it. Even the bugs are quiet."

"You think every town's like this now? This peaceful?"

"Hard to say. I bet the bigger cities still make a fair amount of noise. Who knows about New York, L.A.? Hard to imagine Tokyo's gone silent."

Norman reached out and touched a lilac bush as they drove past. He ripped a flower out and smelled its saccharine perfume.

"The Despair must have hit the big cities harder," Norman said. "One suicidal pyromaniac could have gotten himself some cans of lighter fluid and burned New York to the ground with a single match. Who would have stopped him? Who would have bothered to care?"

Pops sniffled and rubbed his nose. "I don't know about that, Norman. You say those people in Seattle still care, don't you? Well, maybe there's some other pockets of folks left who give a damn, too. Heck. There must be."

Pops drove the golf cart through the Swamp Links entrance, keeping to the mowed path Norman maintained. Here the insects were louder, buzzing and chirping along with hundreds of croaking frogs. Grasshoppers smacked against the golf cart's front window, considered its passengers, and flew away.

They passed a sweet-smelling grove of orange trees. The smell of cut grass also hung in the air, a day old but still pungent. The golf cart whirred as it climbed a steep hill, gravity tugging them backward. "C'mon, baby," Pops cooed. "You can do it." At the top of the hill Hole 9 appeared, 350 yards of flat and unassuming land. At the beginning of the hole was a boxy sheet-metal shed. Pops turned the cart off and they stepped out.

Pops patted the cart's hood. "Stay out of trouble, now."

They grabbed their luggage and headed over. Pops unlocked the shed's door and slid it open. He flicked on the lights and they went inside.

"Wow, Pops. She looks good."

A small, dark blue propeller plane sat gleaming in the middle of the shed. The plane's wingspan was thirty-four feet and beneath each wing hung a turbine engine. The entire shed smelled like fresh paint and oil. Pops must have been out pretty recently, touching things up.

"Thanks. I'm betting *Jenny* will get us all the way to Seattle on one tank of water," Pops said, running a hand along the plane's smooth metallic nose. "Upgraded the hydrogen converters, now she hardly wastes any fuel at all."

"You think we can make it to Seattle on one tank?"

"Maybe."

"Hope you're right, Pops. I don't really feel like touching ground between here and there."

"Heck no. We're not going to let that happen. Are we, *Jenny*?"

They loaded their bags, dried food, whiskey, and water into the plane's cargo hold and strapped everything down.

Norman went out and yanked the shed's bulky front door open while Pops performed a final visual inspection of his plane. When the old man was satisfied, they climbed into their seats and strapped in. Pops smiled as the twin engines rumbled around them, warming up. He read the console and threw switches. Norman realized that Pops' love of flight was what had kept the old man alive and sane during the last few years, that he must have ignored the Despair by throwing all his energy into his favorite hobby.

The plane rolled slowly out of its small hangar and onto the runway. Pops aimed its wheels straight down the flat, grassy runway and slowly pushed the accelerator lever forward. The plane picked up speed and the golf course became a blur. The front of the plane tilted upward, lifted off the ground, and then they were flying, the lift's g-force pressing them back into their seats.

When they reached flying altitude, Pops leveled out the plane. Norman unbuckled his seat belt and ducked into the cargo hold. He found a large Tupperware box and hauled it up front. They ate dried jerky and apples as they watched the green landscape pass below them. The old Southern states had blurred into one mass of forest. No artificial lights, and nothing moved on the pale freeways. The Southern landscape was dense and remote. It could have been the landscape of any jungle in the world if not for the plane's radar maps, which showed a moving blip across an electric red outline of Florida as they soared above so much potential trouble with such astounding ease.

5

Pops asked Norman if he remembered a woman named Maureen Burks. They'd been in the air for over an hour now, the plane's twin engines rumbling as they passed more highways, lakes, and abandoned towns. The clouds had broken up. Opal blue sky and emerald green earth stretched as far as they could see, and the effect was hypnotic.

"No. Why?"

Pops pushed his eyeglasses up the bridge of his nose. "She used to babysit our kids. Back when Helen still worked as a secretary and couldn't be with them during the day. Maureen was one hell of a woman back then. Feisty as hell, she could keep up with a dozen kids and still smile at the end of the day. Optimistic, too. You could hand her lemons and she wouldn't just make lemonade, she'd make hard lemonade, grill up some steaks, and throw a party the neighborhood would talk about for years. That was Maureen for you.

"Well, the Despair had been going for maybe two weeks

when I decided to take a walk around the neighborhood to clear my head and make sure nobody we knew was doing anything foolish. Things looked pretty normal, more or less, but when I stopped at Maureen's, the place was too quiet for a day-care establishment, and when no one answered the front door, I went around back and entered through the sliding back door. I called out a few times but nobody answered. I went on into the big living room she had. In the living room, lying on their sleeping mats, were about two dozen kids. I knew Maureen had taken in the survivors of a few suicides, but I hadn't known there'd been that many damn fool parents willing to leave their kids alone in the world like that. I also felt like a horse's ass, bumbling into naptime like that and shouting my head off, but then I saw Maureen sitting in the corner of the room and my stomach clenched up.

"Maureen had this pretty red-haired granddaughter, maybe five years old. The little girl was sitting curled up on her grandmother's lap like she was sleeping, too, except a dark ring ran around her neck and I knew without looking any closer the girl was dead, murdered by her grandmother's own hands. Then I saw none of the other kids were breathing either, that the only living people in the room were Maureen and me. I stepped forward with my hands clenched, and I'd never struck a woman before, but I punched Maureen square in the jaw as hard as I could, and when she didn't make a noise, I punched her again. Her eyes gained some focus after that, so I asked her if she knew what she'd done and why.

"She told me ant poison and soda pop at snack time. I asked her why the ringed bruise around her granddaughter's neck, and she told me she'd done that one herself because she was family and it would mean more that way. I told her she'd burn in hell for this, and she told me she knew as much, and then she asked me if I'd be merciful and kill her right then and there, like she'd been merciful and killed the orphan children. I told her she could do the job herself and left her there in the dark, with her granddaughter growing cold on her lap."

Pops glanced from the controls to Norman. "You think I did the right thing by her?"

Norman dropped his head back against the seat. "You mean by not killing her?"

"We didn't know how bad it was back then, remember? I could have shown more kindness."

"She murdered twenty-five children, Pops."

"She thought she was doing them a mercy. Looking back, who's to say she was wrong?"

Norman sighed. "You did what you felt was the right thing, Pops."

"Still," Pops said, flipping a console switch, "I wonder sometimes."

The plane shook slightly as it plowed through a rough pocket of air. Norman gripped the arms of the copilot's seat a little tighter until the turbulence passed and the plane leveled out again. The sun peeked out from behind a distant cloud and Norman had to shield his eyes with his hand.

"Leaving town's the best idea we've had in the last five years."

Pops nodded.

"I'm starting to feel that way, too."

They'd been in the air for about three hours when they passed over Kansas City. The city appeared intact, more or less, but its freeways were as motionless as anything else they'd seen. Nothing was burning, at least. Norman was about to say something hopeful when an explosion rocked the plane and smoke streamed across its nose. Pops' jaw clenched, its tendons standing out like steel wires beneath his skin.

"Goddamn. Some idiot just fired at us. I think he hit us, too."

"What?"

Computer screens flashed red on the plane's console. One screen, which showed a diagram of the airplane, showed blinking red lights in one of the plane's engines.

Norman tapped the blinking lights with his finger. "Our left engine's on fire, isn't it?"

"Sort of."

The cabin started to grow uncomfortably warm as the skeleton of Kansas City passed rapidly beneath them, a huddled mass of dark buildings in the blue morning light.

Pops shook his head. "Who the hell cares enough to shoot us?"

Another explosion shook the plane. It tilted downward.

"Better get the parachutes, Norman."

"Parachutes?"

Pops moved faster than Norman would have thought possible, unbuckling himself and darting into the cargo hold. Norman unbuckled and followed the old man. They packed some dried food, water, and whatever they could cram from their bags into the cargo pouches Pops had attached to their otherwise standard-issue parachutes.

"Keep your arms near your sides," Pops shouted above the roar that now came at them from all sides. "The parachutes will open on their own. Land feetfirst, with a bend in your knees. Roll into the fall."

Pops yanked open the plane's cargo door. Wind swept into the cabin, and the rush of it almost knocked Norman backward. Pops walked up to the roaring gap, waved back at Norman, bent over until his body was coiled, and leaped from the plane. Norman closed his mouth against the smoke and wind and stepped forward. He coiled his legs the way Pops had done, and before he could think more about it, he dove forward into the air.

He fell like a coin dropping into a pond.

Norman's descent was surreal, like a computer simulation of skydiving. Greens, browns, and blues everywhere. Air buffeted Norman until it filled his every pore, choking him with cold oxygen he could not breathe in fast enough.

So much air.

Air on top of air.

And the view . . .

He wished Jordan could see all this. "See those tiny trees?" Norman would say to her, pointing them out to her. "See those teeny buildings, those little streets? They're so small now. Everything is so small. Why did you let the world bother you so much, if it's actually so small?"

Norman landed hard on the edge of a wheat field. He tried to tuck and roll, but the landing still hurt as he rolled in a series of clumsy somersaults. When he finally came to a stop, he lay gasping on his back, the parachute spread around him like a pair of flattened wings. He breathed in the smell of damp mud. And breathed again. When he was satisfied he was still alive, Norman got to his feet despite the heavy drag weight of the opened chute. In the distance he could see smoke and what was probably the fiery remains of their plane. The wheat field in front of Norman went on for miles, already tall for springtime and gone to seed. A shape appeared in the nearest field, wading through the wheat.

Norman waved, and the shape waved back.

Norman sat back down. The sun peeked out from beneath a patch of clouds. Pops made his way over, dragging his parachute behind him like a puffy tail.

"Well, that was some fun, wasn't it?"

Norman rubbed his face in his hands. "We weren't invisible, Pops. Whoever shot us down is going to come after us."

"Probably. But this is big country."

"Big country?"

Pops spread his arms wide and grinned. "Big."

PART TWO

Lowland

6

Norman and Pops rolled up their parachutes, slipped them on like makeshift backpacks, and hiked across the field. They skirted the area where their plane had crashed. Eventually, they came to a paved road and started down it without speaking, headed west. Tall, brown weeds blocked their view of anything but the road behind them and the road ahead of them. When Norman breathed deeply, he could smell recently melted snow.

A pheasant ran up from the ditch on their left, darted across the highway, and disappeared into the ditch on their right.

Pops sighed. "We should have packed guns."

"We'll be okay."

"Maybe, but it's a long walk to Seattle from here."

Norman patted the old man on the back. "We'll come across a vehicle that runs. Our luck can't be all bad."

Around noon they came to a car that had veered into the

ditch and crashed into a solitary tree. The car's windows had all been broken, and a man's skeleton still sat in the driver's seat, dressed in the tattered remains of a faded black suit. Cobwebs hung on the roof of the car, over its steering wheel, and swathed the skeleton itself. Norman and Pops munched on dried venison as they peered into the car.

"Maybe he was a salesman who got tired of traveling," Pops said, smacking his lips as he chewed.

"No," Norman said. "Look at that black suit. He was probably on his way to a funeral and couldn't take it anymore. Maybe his wife had already killed herself, and it was her funeral he was going to."

Pops shook his head. "I don't think so, Norman. I think he was the kind of guy who needed to see things through. I'm sure he would have attended the funeral first."

"Any way to salvage the car?"

Pops went around to the front of the car, where a good portion of the grill was still wrapped around the tree. Mushrooms had sprouted on the car's hood. The tree was bent slightly forward, as if growing into the car.

"No, sir," Pops said, frowning. "This car is as dead as the man driving it."

"Guess we better keep walking, then."

At dusk they stopped for the night. They left the highway and waded through twenty yards of weeds to the edge of another wheat field gone to seed. Norman's feet swelled in his boots and his skin was feverish with sunburn. He shrugged off his pack and collapsed onto the ground. He couldn't remember the last time he had gone camping. In college? High school? Never a big fan of the Great Outdoors, Norman usually preferred the Great Indoors, with its electricity and climate control. What happened when their supply of water and jerky ran out? Hunt game? What would they hunt with?

Norman sat up in the grass. Pops massaged his own swollen feet as the sky darkened. His toenails had turned purple. "Helen would laugh to see us now, wouldn't she? Two wide-eyed fools stuck on the east edge of Kansas."

"Well, at least there aren't any mosquitoes."

"Too early for skeeters around here. Still springtime. The skeeters, they'll come a little later."

The stars came out, thick and clear in the darkening sky. They unrolled their parachutes and put on whatever extra clothing they had managed to grab off the plane. Norman wrapped his parachute around him and waddled into the wheat field, collapsing onto the most comfortable-looking spot he could find. He heard Pops doing the same nearby, and in a few minutes the old man was snoring.

Norman counted stars until he couldn't keep his eyes open any longer. His sleep was deep and dreamless, but in the middle of the night he was woken by the sound of howling. Dogs. Abandoned by their masters, they now traveled unchecked across America, alone or in packs, always looking for food, food, and more food. Perhaps the dogs had caught their scent along the road, could smell the dried meat in their packs. Now he and Pops were going to die here in Kansas, torn to shreds and bleeding in a small section of this ratty wheat field. He should not have gone fishing that morning. It would have been better to die with Jordan curled up in bed, coaxing each other into one last shared nap. Why hadn't she told him what she was going to do? Didn't she think he'd understand? How could she have been so selfish?

"You hear that, Norman?" Pops whispered from his patch of darkness. "They're howling like mad."

"Yeah, I hear 'em."

"Never heard a dog howl like that before. I'd say the sound was almost beautiful, if only it didn't make me want to crap my pants."

"A lot of things are like that," Norman said, and turned over into the nylon folds of his parachute. The dogs kept howling and Norman thought of his mother, who'd killed herself early on, during the first week of the Despair. Back then the world still thought the whole thing was some sort of strange epidemic, maybe a virus released by a pissed-off terrorist somewhere. Everyone still kept pretty close tabs on each other. People phoned each other every day to make sure their friends were feeling positive. Internet contact was still maintained with vigilance.

There hadn't been any visible signs of depression. At least, Norman couldn't remember any. His mother had been healthy. She got along well with her husband. She still went to her book club and poker night. She still played piano when Norman came across town to visit, still smiled as she offered him her famous ice-cold lemonade. Norman had no idea that his mother was about to drive her car into a highway underpass at seventy-five miles per hour. No idea she had thought about leaving them at all.

But she had.

Norman's mother hadn't worn a seat belt and was absolutely splattered against the underpass, what remained of her body flecked with stone and Duracrete. Norman's father went to identify the body in a morgue two towns away and returned wide-eyed and distant. He reported that the morgue was so full of bodies a long waiting line ran outside it, filled with other stunned suicide survivors. Norman's father had waited three hours to point at a patch of his wife's bloodied face, declare, "That's her, Officer," then be pushed on through as the winding line grew behind him.

The next day they came to a town. At least, it was an attempt at a town. The homes were spaced far apart, separated by overgrown lawns and rusty chain-link fencing. No tall buildings. Main Street consisted of a small church, a dusty fuel station, and a crumbling restaurant.

"This place looks deserted."

"Hopefully it is," Norman said. "I don't really feel like chatting with anyone today. Let's find a car and get the hell out of here."

They'd only been searching for a few minutes when a man and a woman burst out of a cream-colored house and ran toward them, waving their arms. The woman was thin and pale, the man fat and rosy-cheeked. The fat man stopped a few yards away and raised a hand. "We've been waiting for you all day," he huffed. "We think he's been dead since the middle of the night. Margo and I were worried you had somehow forgotten about us."

Without waiting for a reply, the couple ushered Norman and Pops along. They power walked down one street of plain, dilapidated houses, turned, and trotted down another street. "We've been watching you for a few minutes," the thin woman called Margo said. "At first we weren't sure if you were really who we thought you were, since you're not dressed in black and all. But then I told Herbert, "Herbert, why do you think they'd be wearing black anymore? It's spring now, and if they're on foot, they'd be getting mighty hot in black clothes. Besides, maybe they're trying to spruce up their image with more normal-looking outfits, letting people get to know 'em better and such. Not that there are too many people left to know around here!"

Margo laughed shrilly and pointed toward a row of houses.

"They live over there, boys. We are certainly glad you've come. We were worried that he was going to start, you know, smelling soon. We haven't buried a fly for years and wouldn't know where to start anymore. Would we, Herbert? I don't know where our spades are. They've probably gone to rust, I bet, like everything else in our garage!"

Margo gave another shrill laugh. Norman felt a headache coming on, but Pops smiled at the woman's chatter.

"Now please use your inside voices," Margo said, abruptly dropping her voice to a whisper as they walked up the front steps of a sagging two-story. "The daughter is still very sensitive to her father's passing. She's always been sensitive, you know, but I think this one has really broken her little heart."

Norman opened his mouth to speak, but the absolute silence of the house stopped him. The living room appeared carefully arranged and lived in. A vase of dried sunflowers and cattails sat on the fireplace mantel. An orange afghan lay in the lap of a leather recliner. Two abandoned coffee mugs rested in the center of a coffee table otherwise covered with books.

"He's upstairs," Herbert whispered. "The girl found him yesterday in the bathtub. The poor soul slit his wrists. I took his body out of the tub and cleaned it up some. Then Margo dressed him and we put him in bed."

Margo wrung her hands. "Herbert almost threw his back out lifting him, the poor dear."

The couple led the way upstairs, holding hands like children walking through an unknown neighborhood at dusk. Norman and Pops followed. Clearly, the couple somehow thought he and Pops were Collectors, as ludicrous as it seemed, and Norman was finding it hard to disappoint them.

Everyone stopped in a small hallway. Margo knocked on a

closed door and, hearing no response, opened it and went inside. After a short pause she reappeared outside the door, smiling like a magician about to reveal a fantastic new trick.

"You can go in now, gentlemen."

"I don't know—"

Norman clasped Pops on the shoulder.

"It's all right," Norman said. "Please stay out here while we assess the situation, folks."

Norman led the way into the room. The blinds were drawn, but he could make out a dresser, book-crammed shelves, and a bed pushed against the far wall. A man lay on top of the bed, his hands folded on his chest. A girl sat hunched beside the bed in a wooden chair, her skinny elbows resting on her knees. She had long, dark hair and looked about eleven years old.

"Howdy, miss," Pops said. "Sorry to disturb you."

The girl glared at them from beneath her bangs. She had hazel brown eyes and a deep wrinkle across her forehead, as if she'd been thinking something over for a good long while.

"You're Collectors?"

Norman shook his head. "No. Your neighbors think we are, but we're only drifters, passing through."

The girl's eyes narrowed as she turned to the window blinds.

"Well, they'll be here soon enough, anyway."

7

The dead man's daughter watched Pops and Norman as they stood around the deceased's bed, drinking whiskey from a flask. Herbert and Margo were gone, having declined to take part in the impromptu wake. They seemed annoyed by Pops and Norman's casual, wait-until-morning version of corpse removal (not as efficient a system as they had come to expect, Norman supposed).

Pops peered behind the dim room's window shades. "If I recall correctly, Norman, the last time the Collectors came you dusted off your shotgun. You aren't thinking about pulling a stunt like that again, are you?"

Norman smacked his lips and handed Pops the flask. "No, don't think so. I left my shotgun at home, anyway."

Norman wondered how long it would take the Collectors to arrive. They didn't always show up right away, and they didn't always travel via helicopter. Sometimes they appeared on foot, many days after a suicide's death. Perhaps he and

Pops could bury the dead man in the morning, before they moved on. Surely the Collectors wouldn't show up *tonight*. This was the middle of the middle of nowhere, and the man had only been dead for less than a day. Hell, maybe they didn't bother with Kansas anymore. It was so empty—

"You killed a Collector?"

Norman and Pops turned to the girl, whom they had forgotten. She sat cross-legged on her small chair, and her dark hair hid most of her face. "I can understand that," she said, pardoning Norman before he could reply. "Maybe I should kill the Collectors that come to take my father. I could use the butcher knife from downstairs. I could hide behind the door when they come in—"

"You could do that," Norman said. "But they'd probably kill you before you could do much damage."

"I'm not afraid to die."

"You're not?"

"Why should I be? How can death be worse than this?"

Norman rubbed his face in his hands. When he cupped his eyes with his palms, white clouds floated across his mind, hanging in his vision like a gathering thunderstorm. First the plane crash, now this peculiar, brown-eyed girl sitting with a dead man at dusk. Already, Florida might as well have existed on another sunnier, far-off planet.

"What's your name?"

The girl stared at him for a minute before she replied, her head tilted slightly, like a bird pondering a worm.

"Zero. My name is Zero."

"Like the number?"

"Yes. Like the number."

"Okay . . ."

"My parents were both math teachers before the Despair," Zero said. "My dad says zero is one of the most important things ever discovered. It makes it possible to add ordinary numbers into really big numbers. It gives a small number more power."

Pops rubbed his hands together and blew into them, though the room wasn't really cold. "Sounds like a smart man, hon."

Zero stood up and leaned over her father, stroking his cheek with the back of her hand. "He is. . . . I mean, he was."

Zero's house ran on a hydroelectric generator similar to the one Norman used back in Florida. He heated up venison from Zero's deep freezer while Pops thawed some frozen corn in the microwave. The smell of food cooking rose from the kitchen and drifted throughout the house, doing battle with the scents of dust and mildew. Zero shuffled into the kitchen, dressed in a grubby pink bathrobe. Dark circles ringed her eyes. She sat down at the table and watched them cook without speaking.

Pops banged the pot of corn with a wooden spoon. "Hello there, miss. How's a dinner of corn and deer meat sound?"

"Sounds like what I eat every day."

"Sure it does," Pops said, grinning. "But after a couple of

days of nothing but venison and water, I'm practically drooling."

"Whatever."

They ate in silence. Norman had three helpings. He hadn't had sweet corn like this in years, maybe ever. Zero's father had been wise to stock his larder like this. Tasty food was a good antidepressant. The more meals you had to look forward to, the more reason you had to get out of bed every day. (Yet, Norman remembered, Zero's father had killed himself anyway. What had tipped the scales for him? Perhaps he had decided that his daughter was old enough to carry on without him anymore, that she would survive if he passed on. Maybe the howling wind coming off the flat prairie had finally gotten to him, child or no child.)

"You two eat like you're starving."

Zero had pulled her dark, tangled hair back in a ponytail. You could see more of her pretty, almond-shaped face now, her high cheekbones and the dark freckles on her nose. Definitely eleven years old. Norman set his fork down on the edge of his plate.

"We haven't had a hot meal in a while. We were flying to Seattle when our plane was shot down."

"Kansas City folks," Zero said, crinkling her nose. "My dad said the city turned pretty rough in the end."

"Yeah," Norman said. "I'm sure it wasn't pretty."

Zero drummed her fingers on the table as a grandfather clock chimed in the other room. The girl cocked her head. "But why are you headed for Seattle? What's there?"

"We heard they're rebuilding," Pops said. "Starting civilization up again. Twenty thousand people, still kicking, and there might be a scientist named Briggs working on a cure for the Despair, too."

"Really? A cure?"

"That's what we heard," Norman said. Zero tucked a strand of dark hair behind her ear. Norman felt a negotiation coming on, and he already knew what the girl was going to ask them. He could see it in the way her fingers twitched on the table with barely contained excitement, the way her eyes darted from Pops to him and back again like someone who's just realized she's hit the jackpot. The only question really remaining was how desperate were they, exactly? An eleven-year-old girl could be a huge liability these days. . . .

"So, you two are basically stranded?"

"We can walk," Norman said. "We have feet."

"It's a pretty long walk, though. And dangerous."

Norman shoveled more corn down and took a drink of water. "Don't worry about us, hon. We'll make do."

Zero tucked her feet up under her and shook out her hair.

"My dad kept a truck running. A big red truck with fully charged fuel cells. You know, I suppose I could dig up the keys and give the truck to you for your trip. It'd get you there and then some."

"That would be mighty sweet of you, miss," Pops said. "Don't you think so, Norman?"

Norman pointed his fork at the girl. "What's your price? A running truck is pretty valuable these days."

"My price? Why do you think I have a price?"

"C'mon, now. Spit it out."

Zero leaned forward over her plate. "Take me with you to Seattle. I've always wanted to see the ocean." Zero leaned back again in her chair and stretched her arms. "Heck, I've always wanted to see any place at all that wasn't Kansas."

8

Another clear Midwest morning. The body of Zero's father had been collected quietly during the night, and no one saw the Collectors come and go. No one spoke about the removal as they packed Zero's truck, filling its bed with everything they could possibly need on the open road. This included three sleeping bags, pillows, matches, silverware, first-aid kit, venison jerky, water, rope, a hunting rifle, extra clothes, and an old road map (the household electrical generator was too big, or else they would have added that, too). Norman and Pops secured the cargo with cords and tied a tarp over the truck's bed.

Margo and Herbert came out to see them off. While Herbert shook hands with Zero and Pops, Margo made her way to Norman with her puffy lips pursed. "I don't like this, Mr. Norman. It doesn't seem right, a young girl going off with two strange men."

"We're not that strange, are we?"

Margo's face crinkled as if she'd been squirted with lemon juice. "You know what I mean, smarty. I don't care if you are Collectors, a young lady shouldn't be traveling by herself these days. We've heard all kinds of stories about rape, murder, and worse."

Norman coughed. "Listen, lady. We're not Col—"

"I don't want to hear it," Margo snapped. "You could be lying through your teeth. Leave the girl here, with us. Herbert and I had a daughter of our own, once. We could raise her."

"Zero's already raised," Norman said, shading his eyes from the morning sun. "She's going to do what she's going to do."

"She's eleven years old!"

Norman shrugged and glanced at Zero. "No one who was born before the Despair is a kid anymore. Not really."

Margo bit her lower lip. Herbert came over and shook Norman's hand, wishing him a safe journey. Norman thanked him and got into the truck with the others. He'd drive first, with Pops in the passenger seat and Zero between them. The truck gurgled to life, and Margo and Herbert stood back as the truck pulled out. Norman caught a glimpse of Margo in his rearview mirror, looking small and angry beside her waving husband. "Poor Herbert," Norman said, steering them down the road. Zero ordered the truck's automated windows to roll down and they complied. Wind filled the cab, drowning out small talk as they threaded their way down broken roads. They passed the occasional house, its windows broken, and innards exposed. Norman wondered if dogs slept in the houses at night, competing for space with bats, termites, and whatever else crawled in through the broken screen doors.

The on-ramp to I-70 was clear of debris, and the cracked Duracrete pavement thumped beneath their wheels as Norman pushed the truck up to a giddy thirty-five miles per hour. Zero smiled for the first time Norman could re-member.

"You know what, guys? This is already the farthest I can remember traveling in my whole stinking life."

Norman grinned and pushed the truck up to forty. They drove with the sun at their backs and discovered that the in-terstate was in surprisingly good condition after the years of neglect. It had buckled in spots, but for the most part Nor-man was able to keep the truck moving at a steady clip, right up until Topeka.

The old capital of Kansas had seen better days. Most of Topeka had burned down, and the rest of it was crumbling. The city appeared so dark and unappealing they didn't bother to stop and get out. Here, the interstate was clogged with wrecked cars, and it took three hours to weave through the city's unchanging traffic. Norman drove slowly as Zero told her story:

"When the Despair started I was six years old. It was my birthday, actually, and my parents were having this big party on our lawn. Everybody I knew was there and I couldn't believe so many people could be at our house, drinking punch and eating grilled hot dogs and laughing. All of this was for me, for my birthday. We had chocolate cake, and after I finished my first piece, I went back inside to get another one off the kitchen table. My parents were in the kitchen, too, making coffee and tea. They were watching a reporter on the TV monitor, and their faces were so sad I wanted to cry.

"On TV they showed this huge garbage heap, piled thirty or forty feet high. It was strange because there was a lot of clothing in the garbage heap. Japanese police officers swarmed around the garbage pile, and when the camera zoomed in, I saw the faces. People faces. I screamed and ran to my mother. She picked me up but kept watching the TV monitor. I burrowed my face into her shoulder but I could still hear the announcer say how at this Tokyo nightclub pills had suddenly appeared and been passed around the club. He said all the people had taken the drug together, all at once, and it had been poison. They had all killed themselves on purpose.

"That was the first time I ever heard the word *suicide*. At six years old it's a little hard to figure out death by itself, but suicide was even harder to understand. Why would anyone want to stop moving, to stop breathing and eating and dancing? As the Despair began and more people died, I got more confused. My parents couldn't answer my questions, and we watched almost everyone in our town die out. If you went down the street to borrow a cup of sugar, you walked into your neighbor swinging from the ceiling. If you went into your backyard to play, you might see someone staggering across your lawn, shouting at the sky as blood poured from their wrists. And then the Collectors started showing up. . . ."

Zero shuddered. Norman rolled up his window.

"After Mom hung herself in our attic, Dad and I didn't go anywhere. Dad put a tall wooden fence up around our backyard so I could play without seeing anything weird. We got along pretty good, under the circumstances, and Dad taught me things people used to learn at school. We had a big library of books in our house and I read most of them. I liked to ask my dad questions about the old days, when there used to be cities filled with people and you could do a million different things, like go to museums and the movies and walk around, window-shopping and eating ice cream.

"I could tell my dad was still sad, though, especially when we went through old photo albums that had Mom in the pictures. Sometimes I wondered if he loved her more than me, but then I realized it was a different kind of love. It was the kind of love you read about in Shakespeare. Romantic love. And I guess that sort of love must be a really bad thing after your lover dies, because my father started drinking more, his eyes always red and blurry. I tried to hide the liquor bottles, but he always found them. I started pouring the booze down the drain when he was sleeping. He never got mad at me for dumping out his booze, though, just went into town and found more. Now I wish he would have gotten mad, would have told me to go to hell and slapped me."

Zero stopped speaking. They all stared ahead at the road, flat and shimmering in the sunlight. Plains, and more plains.

Zero put her hand on Norman's shoulder. "Did you really kill one of the Collectors, Norman?"

Norman squeezed the steering wheel. "Yes. I did."

Zero smiled and patted his shoulder. "Then I think you're going to save the world."

They drove beyond the Topeka city limits and continued until they reached a rest stop. The rest stop consisted of a long strip of parking lot and a squat, gray building surrounded by weeds and picnic tables. The rest stop was set back from the road, hidden from the interstate by a dense wall of artificially planted evergreens. More trees surrounded the rest stop itself, and Norman drove the truck over the parking-lot curb and deep into the woods to conceal it. They dragged a picnic table out of the weeds and ate lunch. The trees rustled with the wind, and patches of sunlight and shadow fell around them, always changing, always moving.

After lunch Norman went to the edge of the woods to pee, and as he stood there, exposed, he heard engines roaring toward them in the distance. He zipped up and ran back to the picnic table.

"We've got visitors coming."

They pushed the picnic table into the weeds and ran into the trees. The rumble of engines grew louder as they dropped to the forest floor among the mossy branches and moldering leaves. Pops coughed as the first flash of chrome appeared in the parking lot. "Motorcycles. Nice ones, too." Norman wondered if he had hidden their truck well enough as bike after bike roared into the rest area's parking lot. Norman counted nine motorcycles in all. The riders wore bulky leather clothes, tinted helmets, and had plenty of firearms. One of the bikers shouted, pointing back at the road.

"They're looking for us," Pops whispered. "I bet they're the bastards that shot down *Jenny*."

"Shhhh."

After a few long minutes of shouting the bikers started circling the parking lot again. The bikers gunned their engines and took off. Norman breathed deeply as the gang roared into the distance, most likely rocketing west again down Interstate 70. He pushed himself off the ground and helped Pops to his feet. Zero joined them.

"They're searching for you guys, aren't they?"

"Probably," Norman said.

"So what should we do?"

"Hope like hell they don't find us."

Pops nodded. "I concur."

That night a series of plaintive, high-pitched howls sounded in the distance as they camped out in the truck. Zero sprawled out in the truck's cab, deeply asleep, while Pops and Norman tossed and turned in the truck's bed.

"Poor dogs," Pops muttered, sitting up in his sleeping bag

and looking beyond the truck bed, as if the old man could actually see in the thick darkness. They had parked a few miles off the interstate for the night, in the yard of an abandoned farm and grain depot, and a row of grain silos loomed over the truck like shadowy sentries. Norman was glad to at least have buildings surrounding them, efforts of combined steel and concrete that proved people had once lived and worked here, that Kansas hadn't always been a land of ghosts and wild dogs.

Pops lay back down and Norman closed his eyes. It felt as if he were sinking through the truck and into the ground below it, dropping to the center of the earth. The dogs howled all night.

9

Pops and Norman rose with the sun. They found a fresh-water well, old-fashioned hand pump and all, in front of the farmhouse. Norman pumped water into a rusty tin pail and handed the pail to Pops.

"Lazy man's shower?"

"Thank you," Pops said, taking the bucket from him. "I smell like a pig and a skunk combined, with a little horseshit thrown in."

Norman returned to the truck while Pops bathed. Zero was still asleep in the cab, curled up in the truck's front seat with her arms hugging a balled-up sweatshirt. Her brow was furrowed, as if she were trying to solve a problem in her sleep. Norman got a bar of soap, two towels, and a change of clothes out of the truck bed and headed back to the pump.

He stopped inside the front yard, at first unable to compre-hend exactly what he was seeing. Pops stood at the water pump, dressed only in his underwear and sunglasses. A dozen wild dogs surrounded the old man in a snarling ring, a motley collection of Great Danes, Labradors, German shepherds, and golden retrievers. Each dog was covered in scars and their rib bones protruded through their matted fur. They growled at the old man but kept a few yards back.

Pops lifted the rusty pail above his head and shook it. "C'mon, fleabags! Who wants this rammed down their throat?"

Norman winced. Pops would probably last about ten seconds after the dogs attacked, and that was a favorable estimate. Norman needed to get the old man out of the ring quickly, before he was nothing but a pile of mangled bones and chewed-up boxers. No time to go back for the truck. Norman grabbed a heavy branch off the ground and stepped toward Pops.

"You better put your clothes back on, big guy."

The growling dogs turned to Norman. Pops jumped into his blue jeans and pulled a T-shirt over his head. He slipped his shoes on so hastily that he tripped over his feet, almost falling into a golden Lab with a torn ear. The pack of dogs turned back to the fumbling old man, then back to Norman, as if trying to decide which human to attack first. Norman planted his feet and gripped the branch like a baseball bat.

"Pops, walk towards me. Slowly, looking straight ahead."

Pops took a step. The dog nearest him, a black Lab with a white muzzle, growled.

"No," Norman said, pointing the branch at the Lab. "Bad dog. Bad dog!"

The Lab backed off. Pops took three more steps. The

stongest-looking dog in the group, the German shepherd, bared his teeth and snarled. Norman raised the branch above his head. "Hey. Back off, asshole."

The shepherd barked and lunged at the old man. Norman brought the branch down as hard as he could. The blow connected solidly with the dog's head and the animal dropped to the ground. Norman roared and swung the branch some more. Half the dogs scattered, but the hungrier half charged. Norman knocked a second one down but the others were on him before he could bring the branch back around. He toppled backward under their weight and felt jaws on his throat, then heard a loud clang and the jaws slipped off. He grabbed a fur-covered throat, thin and sinewy, and squeezed until he felt it crack in his hands. Then another clang and he could hear Pops cursing as the old man wrestled one of the Great Danes to the ground. Norman got to his knees as a golden retriever latched onto his forearm and bit down, hard. Norman bellowed and punched the dog with his free hand and punched it again, and when it finally released his arm, he picked the dog up and slammed it headfirst into the ground. Its neck crunched and the dog went limp in his arms and he threw it away from him, toward the more cowardly dogs.

Norman staggered to his feet, arm bleeding, and watched the cowardly dogs fall on the retriever's limp body and rip it apart. Pops had won his own fight, too, and Norman helped the old man to the edge of the yard, where they stood gasping. After they finished devouring the golden retriever, the cowardly dogs converged on the remaining fallen dogs and, even while the fallen dogs still breathed, dug into their throats and ate their entrails in the morning light, blood matting their steaming muzzles as they chewed.

Pops leaned on his knees, sucking air into his lungs. "That's what it's like to be truly hungry. Right there. No sentimental feelings, no anything."

Norman wrapped his hand around his bitten forearm. "Let's get back to the truck."

Luckily, the retriever hadn't torn any tendons in Norman's forearm, and other than a few small cuts, Pops was fine. They cleaned Norman's wound, stitched it up with self-dissolving thread from Zero's first-aid kit, and swaddled it in gauze and tape. The wound burned, but overall, things could have been much worse.

They pulled back onto Interstate 70, heading west. Zero drove. Norman slumped against the passenger door and watched the world through a squint, his gaze sweeping over the roadside underbrush. Zero glanced at him.

"What are you thinking about? Those dogs?"

Norman squinted through the windshield. Kansas was still unfurling in front of them like a gigantic green flag.

"No. Not the dogs."

"What then?"

"Nothing."

"No, you were definitely thinking about something. You were thinking about love, weren't you?"

"Love?" Norman noticed a jittery horse in a passing field. The horse, whose rib cage protruded like skeletal armor, nibbled on a patch of wildflowers. Its round eyes darted in their sockets, as if the horse expected something unpleasant to happen to it at any moment. The horse was probably right.

"You're thinking about your one true love, aren't you? You probably lost her during the Despair, like everyone else, and now you miss her. You miss her like my dad missed my mom. You wonder why she left you alone."

Norman scratched his chin. "Actually, I was thinking about what we were going to have for lunch."

"Ha. Doubt it."

Norman ignored the throbbing in his forearm and fell into a doze. He dreamed of the day his father had passed. By then, Norman's mother had been dead for three weeks. It was mid-August and smoke from the cremation fires hung thick over Florida. The few people in the street kept coughing, their eyes wide and bleary above their surgical masks. All the stores had shut down or were running on skeleton crews. Norman stepped inside the drugstore, still open, all its aisles lit with neon light, but no one worked any of the counters. He picked out a roll of deodorant, put a few dollars on the counter, and went back outside.

"Stay back!" someone shouted.

Norman looked up toward the voice. Across the street, two men stood on the courthouse roof. The courthouse was the tallest building in town, four stories high, but even from this distance Norman could tell that one of the men was his father and the other was Stanley Rapson, his father's best friend. Stanley stood on the building's edge, bending his knees like a diver preparing to enter a pool. Norman's father stood about six feet behind Stanley. On this still day their conversation carried across the courthouse parking lot.

"C'mon, Stan," Norman's father said. "You don't want to do that."

"She's gone, Greg. Did I tell you that? She's killed herself and took the kids with her."

His father took a step closer to Stanley. Norman dropped his shopping bag and ran to the courthouse.

"You splattering yourself on that sidewalk down there isn't going to help anything, either. Why don't you come back with me and talk this over, Stan? We'll have a few drinks."

"I know what you're trying to do, and I appreciate it," Stan said. "I really do. But I want to die, you see? And if I don't do it now, I'll do it tomorrow. Or the next day. You've seen how things are changing. Getting worse every day. They're going to declare martial law. The cemeteries are going to overflow, and then they'll start digging pits. I don't want to end up in some fucking pit, Greg. I'd rather be placed with my family."

Norman reached the parking lot. He could still see Stan, but his father wasn't visible at this angle. Norman wondered what he could do to help. He couldn't catch Stan if he jumped. The man outweighed Norman by a good hundred pounds; he'd crush them both.

"You won't end up in a pit, Stan. This is simply another panic. Remember the Bio Scare? Remember how we all wore gas masks for two months, trembling at every sign of skin discoloration? If we survived that, we sure as hell can survive a bunch of crazy folks killing themselves."

Norman wondered if his father meant what he said. This was the first time since Mom's death he had sounded optimistic. Maybe his father was coming back around, shaking the gloom off.

"Sorry," Stan said, and leaned forward. Norman heard his father curse and suddenly a second man's figure joined Stanley Rapson on the edge of the roof, tackling him from behind. Then they became two dark silhouettes against a golden afternoon sky, their limbs flailing against the air as they plunged down, headfirst. Norman stood motionless as they landed at his feet and splattered across the pavement. Norman slumped down beside the broken men. The bodies twitched as if they might rise again, but they did not. He hugged his knees to his chest and took his father's hand in his own. An ambulance wailed in the distance, but he knew it probably wasn't for the two dead men. He hung his head and wept for a long time.

When he looked up again, Norman found himself surrounded by a ring of gaunt people in dark robes. He had never personally seen the dark robes before, but he had heard the reports. Apparently, they had started showing up everywhere. They took away the suicide dead without a word while everyone stood around and watched. Norman had never been able to understand why the survivors had never fought for their dead, had never rebelled against such a weird practice. Now that it was happening to him, things were different. Really, what did it matter what they did with the bodies? Nothing would bring them back, would it? Nothing at all.

"Who are you?"

"We serve the Source," one of the dark robes answered. "We have come to relieve you of your burden."

Norman blinked. Fresh sirens wailed in the distance. A woman shrieked nearby. He just wanted to crawl into bed and never come out again. The way so many people had already done . . .

No.

He couldn't deal with all this shit right now.

He wouldn't.

Norman turned his back on the broken people and the dark robes and started home, where his lovely wife would be watering the plants and listening to Rachmaninoff. They would sit in their sunny living room and sip lemonade. Nothing, not even the fresh death of his father, would be able to touch him there.

10

What was this?

Birds chirping. Sunlight on his face.

"Is he awake yet, Zero?"

"I think so. His nostrils are really flaring."

"Maybe I should pour water on him. That'll do the trick."

Norman opened his eyes. Blurry light poured in. Zero, kneeling over him, her long hair hanging like curtains around her face.

"Hey! His eyes are open. Hi, Norman. Welcome back to earth."

Norman licked his lips.

"Thirsty?"

"Where are we? Why aren't we moving?"

"Pops thought we better pull off the road for a while. You'd turned sort of pale and we couldn't wake you up. We thought maybe you were in shock. How do you feel?"

Norman sat up. His right arm throbbed and he remembered the dogs.

"I'm fine. We should get going."

Pops kneeled next to Zero, squinting as he checked Norman over. He was chewing a piece of cheatgrass.

"Seattle's not going anywhere, Norman. Your health is more important. I think we should find a house somewhere off the interstate and hole up a few days. Make sure your wound heals properly. You're not going to make it with an infected wing, son. No chance of that."

Norman pushed himself off the ground with his good arm and stood back up. They'd come to another rest stop, one even lonelier and more abandoned than the first.

"You think so, huh?"

"Yes, sir. I do. Besides, maybe that biker gang will get bored and stop looking for us. Two birds with one stone, so to speak."

"Okay. Why not?"

Zero brushed her hair away from her face. "You feeling good enough to travel?"

"I'm fine. Let's go. These rest stops make me nervous."

"Oh, yeah," Zero said. "Me too."

They drove on until they reached the closest exit ramp, where they turned off the interstate and headed in the direction of a small town a quarter-mile distant. The town consisted of two rows of houses, one on each side of the street, and, farther down, a small business district. As they passed the first house on the edge of town an old woman in a blue-

and-white checkered dress ran out from behind a clump of bushes, arms flailing in the air.

Zero tapped the truck's brake. "Whoa. Is she . . . waving?"

Norman squinted through the windshield. The old woman sprinted to the truck, shouting as she waved her arms.

Zero put the truck in park but didn't engage the parking brake. "What should we do?"

"See what she wants," Pops said. "Looks like she's itching to talk pretty bad."

The old woman tripped over a rock and fell on the gravel road. She failed to put her arms out to break her fall and landed hard. A wooden handle stuck out between her shoulder blades. Zero moaned as blood spurted up from the wound.

"Hell," Pops said. "That's a hatchet."

Two little girls scrambled into view. Norman guessed seven or eight years old, but it was hard to tell because their faces were covered with grime and their hair was a wild, tangled mess. The girls, one blond and one brunette, stood over the fallen woman and smiled as the old woman tried to crawl away from them. The brunette grabbed the hatchet's handle and pulled it out of the old woman's back. More blood gushed out onto the gravel.

"What are they doing, Norman, what are they doing . . ."

Pops opened his door, but before he could step down, the brunette buried the hatchet in the back of the old woman's skull. The old woman's neck snapped back, her mouth trying to form words. Then her face fell to the road and she lay still. The brunette attempted to pull the hatchet out again but it was buried too deeply now. The girls turned their faces to the sky, opened their small mouths, and let out a set of piercing screams that made Norman's testicles curl inward.

"Holy damn," Pops said. "Holy damn."

"They killed her," Zero said, putting the truck back into drive. She floored it, heading toward the two screaming girls and their kill. Zero pulled the truck to the left at the last second, narrowly missing the girls with the truck's grille, and whipped back around to face them again. The passenger-side door slammed shut without Pops' help as the truck skidded to a stop.

Norman shook his head. "Zero—"

"They killed her. You saw them do it, Norman. You saw."

The girls did not move. They stood staring at the truck as if they'd never seen one moving before, and Norman realized they probably hadn't. Zero revved the truck's engine.

"Zero, if you hit those girls, we're leaving you here," Norman said. "We don't know the whole story yet."

"They killed that old lady."

"Put the truck in park and give me the keys."

"But—"

"We'll do it, Zero. We'll leave you here."

Zero's chin fell against her chest. Norman put the truck in park himself and turned the engine off. The girls, freed from the truck's rumbling spell, abandoned their kill and sprinted off down the street toward the center of town. Pops let out a loud sigh. Mourning doves cooed from the trees and a dog barked in the distance. A second old woman stepped out from behind another clump of bushes, also dressed in a blue-and-white-checkered sundress.

"More company," Norman said. "What a town."

The old woman ignored the truck and bent over the dead woman's body. She rolled the body onto its back and placed a white handkerchief over the dead woman's face. She stood back up, straightened her dress, and waved to the truck. Norman noticed the waving woman looked exactly like the dead woman.

"Oh my," Pops said.

"Yeah," Norman said. "Twins."

Zero bent over and wept softly above her lap, her dark hair spilling onto her knees. Norman's forearm throbbed with smoldering pain. He wished he could go back to sleep for another six hundred miles or so.

"Guess we should go talk to her and see if she wants help," Pops said. "Right thing to do, I suppose."

Norman rubbed his jaw. "Can't we take a pass on this one, Pops? You know, skip a turn?"

The old woman waved to them again, as if maybe they hadn't seen her the first time.

Pops clucked his tongue against his teeth. "It'll be worse if we don't get out, Norman. Somehow, it will be."

"Sure," Norman said. "I thought you'd say that."

The dead sister's name was Eileen, and the living sister's name was Alice. That afternoon they buried Eileen in the backyard of a two-story house that was surrounded on all sides by a high brick wall. The burial went swiftly because three burial plots had already been dug out, each the requisite six feet deep. All that was really needed was to lower Eileen into the grave, shovel dirt on top of her, and stand back while Alice recited the Lord's Prayer and then, with bleary eyes, invited them all into the house for tea. They accepted Alice's invitation and went inside.

No one asked about the third grave.

"We never killed ourselves because it didn't seem right. All those years of living behind us, why end it all with our own hands? Those girls that killed Eileen, bless her dear old heart, were local children from town here. Wild ones, we call them. All of them born right before or during the Despair. Oldest can't be more than nine years. They live in the high school together and do as they please, day and night. Used to be they caused the normal sort of trouble. Vandalism. Harassing animals. Then they started killing animals. Killing each other and anyone foolish to be caught napping while they were on the prowl. Vicious little monsters, is what they are.

"Of course, what else can you expect? Their parents are all dead, every single last one of them. It was the local sheriff who took them in. Hal Harrington. Started collecting them, if you will. Hal claimed it would make the most sense if they all lived together, in one location, where the law would look after them. Ha. Isn't that a kicker? Law. Hal Harrington knew about as much about justice as he did astrophysics. We don't have any proof, but it's a safe bet old Hal turned that high school into hell's own shadow. Created a little kiddy harem, is what he did. Buggered 'em all until they turned as rotten as he was.

"Course a man like Hal Harrington has his limits, too. What he can live with over the long haul. He went last fall. Jumped into the school's incinerator, they say, holding a five-year-old boy in his arms, like maybe he could ride piggyback on that poor boy's soul as it rose to heaven. Even evil has its limits.

"Eileen and I were able to hold on as long as we have because of Joey. That's our grandson. Had Down's syndrome, but he got on alright. Strong as a bull, that boy, and would walk barefoot across glass to make you happy. He was able to get food for us all these years. Kept the wild ones away, too. Joey could holler something fierce if he got scared or nervous, and the only time they tried to scale the wall and attack the house, he threw them back onto the other side like they were bags of trash.

"Four days ago Joey went out to food hunt and didn't come back. Not by dinnertime, not by dark. He'd never done that before, being scared of the dark as he was. The next day Joey still didn't come back, or the third day, and by today Eileen and I were tearing our hair out, we were so worried. This morning Eileen decided one of us should go scouting to see if she could find him and bring him home. I was the one with a gimpy leg, so she went out and I stayed home, cowering behind the window curtains like the piss-smelling cat I've become. And I take it you all saw how well that little expedition turned out, didn't you?"

Alice pushed her cup of tea away from her place at the table and stood up.

"Well, thank you for listening to an old woman, and thanks for helping with the body. You're welcome to stay as long as you like, and judging by looks, I'd say some rest would be a welcome thing for all of you. Plenty of bedrooms, linens in the closet. I'm going to bed."

Alice shuffled out of the kitchen. Norman, Pops, and Zero stayed behind to finish their tea and talk the situation over. They decided to stay with Alice for a week to help out and give Norman's arm time to heal, and within the hour the house was filled with black, exhausted sleep.

Alice's house had a small balcony on the second floor. Pops liked to spend the day sitting up there, watching over the town with a pair of binoculars. He tracked the movements of the local kids, or "the wild ones." They came sniffing around outside the brick wall surrounding Alice's house a few times a day, usually carrying baseball bats and knives. Pops would shout at them and wave his rifle in their direction until they got the idea and ran off.

Their truck was stored in Alice's garage, and twice a day Norman went out to make sure it hadn't been disturbed. The vehicle made him dream of Seattle, of the Pacific Ocean rolling in on a sandy beach and wading through the chilly surf, pant legs rolled up. They'd all go out and have a beach picnic. Eat sandwiches and drink soda pop. Life wouldn't be perfect, but it'd be way past tolerable.

The day after their arrival, Alice noticed Norman's bitten forearm and got out a bottle of hydrogen peroxide, fresh bandages, and a tube of first-aid ointment. She removed the old, blood-crusted wrap and gently examined the bite. Pops' stitch work was clean and the wound was healthy enough, more pink than scarlet. After the old woman cleaned, anointed, and wrapped the wound up again, Norman could already feel the itch that meant healing.

"You'll be on the mend in no time," Alice said. "That dog sure wanted a hunk of you, didn't he?"

"It was starving."

"Lots of folks hungry these days. Hard to blame those wild ones for going mad. Must be as hungry as those dogs. No mother to look after them, no one to cook them dinner at night. Grabbing anything they can and swallowing it down."

"You think they're cannibals?"

Alice shook her small, bird-like head. "Not yet, I don't think. But they aren't far away. They don't remember much of the old days. They don't recall civilization, what it was like to wake up every day not worried about staying alive. Gone feral."

"The next generation," Norman said. "Despair's children."

Zero spent the days reading and sitting with Alice. Alice taught the girl how to knit, and they spent hours in the living room together, the light clicking sound of aluminum needles rising between them like a coded conversation. Sometimes

Pops would leave his balcony post to chat with the ladies, and Norman would take over for the old man. Norman enjoyed watching over the surrounding neighborhood because it reminded him of sitting on his front porch back in Florida. Norman's vigils were always peaceful, and it was easy to believe things were as calm in Kansas as they'd been back home. He thought about Jordan and tried to remember what she looked like in a variety of outfits, in a variety of situations, and on a variety of days. How her lips curled to the right when she smiled, how soft her neck had felt against his cheek.

Each day after dinner in Alice's house they cleared off the dining room table and played cards. Alice didn't have a well-stocked larder, but she did have a good supply of liquor, and the adults would slowly get drunk as the evening progressed, and whenever they heard something howl or scream in the neighborhood, they all drank a shot. The later it got, the less they spoke, cards slapping on the table, someone dimming the lights while pencils scratched meaningless game scores on yellowed paper, and if Norman tried to focus too hard on the room around him, tried to pay too much attention, he could almost feel all their shared ghosts pressing down, hanging around the fringes of their card game like a rapt casino audience. So many to remember: Zero had her parents, Alice her twin sister and grandson, Pops his lost wife and children, and of course Jordan, beautiful, desperate Jordan, a woman worth killing a man for, even in death.

All of this and a card game, too.

The week passed quickly. Norman's wound hadn't totally healed, but it was on its way. They hadn't seen any Collectors, but everyone agreed they'd started to feel uneasy and that it was time to get moving. On their last night in town, after the card game finished and Zero went upstairs to bed, Pops and Norman sat up with Alice and helped her finish a bottle of brandy.

"Who would have thought it would turn out like this, boys?" Alice asked them, looking up at the room's ceiling. "All that human history and work, and here we all are, struggling just to keep sucking air? Makes me feel tired. Hellishly tired."

"Come with us, Alice," Pops said. "It won't be safe here for you anymore. That brick wall won't keep them out for long once we're gone."

Alice snorted. "Won't be any safer for you on the road, Pops, and a gimpy geezer like me would only slow you down. Besides, I don't want to leave the house. Maybe Joey will come back someday, grinning with some miraculous story."

"I don't think that's going to happen, Alice," Norman said. "I'm sorry."

Alice nodded. "I knew all this would end eventually. The wild ones are getting older now. Smarter, too. My grandson wasn't going to avoid them forever. Not with how he was wired."

Pops took a drink and frowned. "You don't have much food left, Alice. What'll you do when you run out?"

"Go to the grocery store, stupid."

Alice cackled and took a long pull of brandy. She licked her lips and stood up from the table. "I appreciate your concern, gentlemen, but the Lord's will be done. I'm ninety-three and too old to go anywhere except heaven, and we'll see about that. See you in the morning."

"Good night, Alice," Pops said. The old woman shuffled off to bed. In a few minutes they could hear her snoring loudly in her bedroom, but neither of them made a move to get up.

"Well," Pops said, "she's determined."

"Soon as we're down the road, those kids are going to drop over that wall," Norman said. "They'll probably take their time with her, too. Let their sadistic little impulses really fly."

"I know it. It was that boy keeping them away this long."

They both took a drink. The room spun on a familiar axis. Norman wondered what the Collectors were up to tonight, how much work they had in Kansas and elsewhere.

Pops pushed his chair back from the table. "I'll take this one, Norman."

Norman held up the bottle of brandy to the light. Through it, everything was colored amber. "Thank you, Pops."

Pops went over to the living room couch and picked up a pillow. He held it against his leg as if it were heavy, like a sledgehammer, and walked into the dark mouth of the old woman's bedroom. A few seconds later, the sound of snoring stopped abruptly and the wind picked up outside.

Norman finished his drink and went out to the garage to get the shovels.

11

It rained hard all the next morning. They drove slowly along the cracked slab of Interstate 70, tires squishing the red, ropy night crawlers that had confused the gray daylight for evening and the interstate for high ground. Norman concentrated on the road, on driving through the fat droplets of rain that drummed against the truck's body like small fingers tapping to get in. Herds of thunderclouds swarmed on the horizon. Lightning zipped down, crackling white, and zipped back up again. Zero had been told that Alice had peacefully passed away during the night in her sleep, and, mercifully, the girl was kind enough not to ask any follow-up questions. Pops sipped steadily from a bottle of whiskey, saying nothing, even when thunder cracked down on them and rattled the truck's frame.

They approached an overpass with a semitruck overturned beneath it, clogging the road with its jackknifed body. Norman drove up the off-ramp at five miles per hour. Water streamed under the truck's tires, and when they got to the top of the overpass, they had a good view of the rain and not much else. The on-ramp west was littered with large stones. Norman put the truck in park.

"Stay in the truck, Zero," Norman said. He and Pops got out, and the sheets of rain instantly drenched them. They slowly rolled the rocks off the ramp. Norman's forearm throbbed but he didn't care. Pops looked sad and old, and Norman didn't care about that, either, he just rolled the rocks out of the way and got back in the truck. He turned the truck's heat on high and Zero handed out towels. They sat watching the rain, waiting to dry off and get warm again as the truck's heater rumbled. Zero shifted in her seat, pulling her legs up beneath her and sitting cross-legged. Two streaks of lightning lit the sky in unison, arcing down into a single point, like the letter *v*.

"Seattle isn't that far away, guys. We're going to make it."

Norman blew into his hands. The truck smelled as if it had been invaded by wet dogs.

"You think so, Zero?"

"Sure. I've got to see the ocean, don't I? No one should ever have to die without seeing the ocean. Right, Pops?"

Pops licked his lips. "Sure, hon. You'll get to see the ocean."

Zero put her arm around the old man's neck and gave him a squeeze. "So cheer up, guys. It's only rain."

Three rainy days later they camped off the edge of the interstate, only fifty miles or so from the Kansas-Colorado border. All of them were exhausted, especially Pops. The old man hadn't slept since leaving Alice's place, and deep patches of purple ringed his eyes, as if they'd been tattooed there. The rain had stopped that afternoon, at least, and the men were able to sleep in the truck bed again after three straight nights of upright dozing in the truck's cab. Norman had never been so happy to stretch out, and he fell asleep with Pops already snoring softly beside him. Norman slept on his back, with a blanket covering his face against the chill. He slept deeply, much longer than usual, and when he woke up, it was already midday and two men were standing in the truck bed above him, armed with shotguns and unsmiling. Norman asked if they were Collectors.

"Worse," one said. "Now get your ass up."

The shotgun men took them to a clearing a few hundred yards away. Amid a circle of parked motorcycles and armed riders stood an enormous man they called the Mayor. The ruddy-faced thug was thick and square, like a retaining wall. He paced in front of them in a heavy, tromping way that threatened shattered windows and bare-fisted violence. This went on for a good while, and with each passing minute Norman was more and more surprised that none of them had yet been shot.

The Mayor stopped pacing. "So, you're Norman."

Norman glanced at Pops.

"What?"

"Norman," the Mayor said. "The guy from Florida."

"Never heard of him," Norman said, coughing into his hand.

The Mayor chuckled from the back of his throat. "Well, well. How the fuck about that. Norman from Florida, standing right here in front of me. You know how long we've been looking for you slippery motherfuckers?"

"Since you shot our plane down?"

The Mayor smiled. "That's right. Since we shot your plane down. And do you know why we did that?"

"Because you're assholes."

The Mayor stopped smiling. "Did you know the Collectors put a bounty on your head, Norman from Florida? With a decent-sized reward?"

"No. I didn't know that."

"The old landline in my office started ringing the other day. Surprised the shit out of me, actually. Didn't even know it still worked. Well, this woman on the other end of the line said a plane might be flying through Kansas City airspace in the next few hours, a small twin-engine, and they'd make it worth our while if we could blow it out of the sky and bring this man from Florida named Norman to them, dead or alive. She offered Kansas City a reward of five hundred pounds of dried venison and twenty functioning generators. Just for catching you, Norman. Why is that?"

Norman kicked a rock with the toe of his hiking boot, sending it skipping across the grass. "Well, there is one thing they might be a little unhappy about."

"What's that?"

"I killed somebody."

The Mayor shrugged.

"I killed a Collector. He was trying to take my wife's body, so I blew his head off."

The Mayor smiled at his gang. "Hell, and I thought I'd heard every crazy goddamned story in the book. Killed a Collector, the man says. Personally, I didn't even know they were human. Thought maybe aliens from outer space, or some shit like that. And you know what else? I think you're lying to me, Norman."

The Mayor pulled out a pistol and aimed it at Norman's forehead. "No. You didn't kill a Collector, Norman from Florida. I bet you did something real nasty instead. Something real bad."

Zero cleared her throat, coiling her legs as if preparing to launch herself at the Mayor. "He did so kill one," she said. "But he isn't proud of it, so stop being such a stupid jerk."

"Zero, stay back. Let the asshole shoot me if he wants."

The Mayor pulled back the pistol's hammer. Norman stared into the gun's shadowed barrel and thought about his wife lying in bed, naked beneath a blanket, and all the desperate others who had died, all of them naked in the end, and he would be just one more naked body, added to the heap.

The Mayor lowered the pistol, a crease denting his broad forehead.

"Damn. Maybe the man is telling the truth, after all."

Norman, Pops, and Zero sat on the hood of their truck as the Mayor's gang debated on the other side of the camp whether to turn Norman in for the Collectors' bounty. A guard had been posted twenty feet away from the truck, a rifle cradled in her arms. "If those jerks decide to give you up," Zero whispered, staring at her nails, "I'm going to scratch their eyes out."

"Yeah," Pops added. "Figure I can get off at least three shots with our rifle before they catch up. Norman, you'll have to use one of the kitchen knives and fight hand to hand. Think they're in the back of the truck. Zero, why don't you go grab the cutlery right now?"

The guard frowned at them and shifted the rifle in her arms.

"No. I don't want to fight," Norman said. "They can have me if they want me. I don't want anyone else to get hurt. That's enough of that."

"But, Norman—"

"No."

The debate continued into late afternoon. Norman took a nap in the back of the truck while his fate was decided. When he woke, the sun was descending below the horizon, casting a golden glow over the truck's bed. Norman felt like staying in the truck bed all evening. He would watch the flat Midwestern sunset, the gradual fade from blazing pink to cobalt blue before the stars emerged in sparkling droves.

Norman's guard stepped up to the truck bed and announced that the Mayor had asked everyone to dinner. Pops, Zero, and Norman went over, accompanied by their guard.

The Mayor's crew had built up a roaring campfire and rolled small boulders around it for chairs. The Mayor was eating grilled venison and potatoes off a paper plate, and he nodded when he saw them. Norman nodded back and sat on a boulder between Pops and a woman with blond, spiked hair. The blond woman offered him a steaming plate of meat and potatoes, and Norman took it, eating with such focus that he could barely concentrate while the Mayor introduced his gang at length, giving not only each member's name but what occupation he or she had held before the Despair, as if those old ways mattered. When the Mayor finished with all the introductions, Norman swallowed his food and cleared his throat.

"So, Mayor, does this sudden burst of friendliness mean you're going to let us go after all?"

The Mayor smiled. "We talked it over this afternoon and decided that it would be wrong to turn you in, Norman. Many of us have wanted to shoot the Collectors ourselves, you know, we just never had the balls."

Norman pushed the food on his plate around. "We all know that if we still had laws, and police to enforce those laws, I'd be behind bars by now. I killed an unarmed human being."

Zero stood up. "But, Norman, you—"

Norman held his hands up. "Don't you start either, honey. You've been reading too many old books."

Zero sat back down. She picked up her plate, and though it was still full, she chucked it into the fire. The plate caught immediately, and the food popped and sizzled before it burned to char.

"You're too hard on yourself, Norman," the Mayor said. "I can tell a man who's too hard on himself from a mile away. I'm like that, too. Thinking things over all the time, trying to decide what I should have done better, how I could have maybe saved that person or this person if maybe I had said the right thing, smiled the right smile. The thing is, you have to let go after a while or else you go crazy. And once you're crazy, you're no good to anybody."

Norman grinned. "How'd you come to such a wise and profound revelation, Mayor?"

The Mayor chuckled. "Now, that's a long fucking story."

Norman took in the raw, hungry faces in the firelight. "It'll be a long night. I don't mind listening."

The Mayor peered out beyond the campfire. Norman wondered where the big man was really looking, what he was really seeing.

"I was a bricklayer," the Mayor said, turning back to the campfire's center. "A mason. Masonry was considered a dying art, even when I started. Technology had improved and construction drones were starting to actually get the job done. They weren't as, well, *artful* as human workers, but they could lift heavier loads, work twenty-four hours a day, and they never formed unions to demand decent health benefits. Pretty soon it got so bad the unions had to lower their standards so humans could still get jobs.

"Well, this pissed me off, as you might expect. I've never been what you'd call 'tolerant,' especially when it came to suits trying to break my balls, so I took matters into my own hands.

I started a company with some guys who were out of work. We made a pretty good go of it at first, taking jobs out in the suburbs where people still didn't like the idea of robotic labor.

"About a year after we started, a company called SBT Construction began hounding my crew. We'd had plenty of competition before, what with all the other human masons trying to scratch out a living, but SBT's crews were mostly drone workers with a minimum of human foremen and repairmen. The SBT crews liked to drive by our residential sites and put on a demonstration for the people in the neighborhood, showing them how much faster and cheaper the drones could do the work for them. There we were, working our sweaty asses off in the scorching sun, and we had to watch those damn robots work like hauling stone was playtime for them.

"I found out who was in charge of SBT Construction itself. I put on my suit and visited his office. I told the president's secretary I was a prospective client, a very rich one, and I think I surprised the president because he didn't have a chance to call security before I beat the living crap out of him."

The Mayor laughed and held his thick, callused hands up to the fire. It had gotten colder and you could see your breath now. A bottle of Scotch was being passed around the campfire. When it reached Norman, he took a healthy pull and hissed the fumes out between his teeth.

"They threw me in prison for assault. Two years without parole. I'd only been in the tank for a few months when signs of the Despair first started showing up in the papers. I liked to read magazines and newspapers in the prison's library, where it was quiet and a guy could breathe without being hassled. I read all about the mass suicide in Tokyo, about how it was so sudden and unexpected, with no evidence of a cult or a pact or anything, and from there I was hooked. I followed the obit section like it was baseball scores, and any article about the new suicides I ripped out when the librarian wasn't looking and taped it into a notebook. I don't know why I was so interested back then. At first it all seemed pretty random, nothing to get worked up about. I suppose it wasn't until all the movie stars in Hollywood began biting the dust that the rest of the world paid much attention.

"At first, the other inmates didn't seem too bothered by the Despair, either. They thought it was sort of funny, the rest of the world suffering while we were locked up safe and sound. Then reports about the inmates' own families started to seep into the prison, and things got ugly. Everything you can imagine a person killing themselves with was confiscated, and a twenty-four-hour lockdown went into effect. That was hell. Everyone pacing up and down their cells. All day long, all night long, like panthers in a zoo. You could hear every little thing. The hum of the air-conditioning system was like a roaring waterfall. Guys started finding new and interesting ways of killing themselves. The prison staff, which was already running low in the numbers department, couldn't keep up with all us damn lemmings."

The Mayor made a croaking sound that Norman assumed was laughter.

"After almost everybody in the prison was dead, a guard let

me out of my cell, handed me a set of fresh clothes, and wished me luck. The guard, the last breathing one in the whole damn building, told me that he was fixing on going out either by hanging or sleeping pills, and that he couldn't decide which. His eyes were so glassy, so damn spooky, that I punched him with a right cross and ran like hell. I mean, I fucking sprinted out of that damn prison, the whole time thanking God that I hadn't been left to die locked up and alone.

"Outside, I found a fucked-up version of the America I had left. Cars and trucks were parked everywhere, with no rhyme or reason, and some had been set on fire like plastic funeral pyres. Hardly any people around, and the ones you did see were babbling and weeping so much you couldn't get any sense out of them. They were zombies. Harmless, brokenhearted zombies. They talked about brothers and sisters and girlfriends and fathers and every damn person they knew, and then they talked about how each person had decided to die. I tried to make some of them eat, cooked them the best damn meals I ever made in my life, but the poor bastards couldn't choke a thing down. Folks grew so thin I couldn't stand it; I was as wide as six of them put together. And threatening the zombies to snap out of it did no good, either. They weren't afraid of anything, man. Live electrical cables could fall down at their feet, hissing and sparking and shit, but they'd step over it like it was a sleeping puppy dog.

"On top of all this, the Collectors were already in full swing. They cruised the streets in minivans without windows, in semitrucks, in long, gray hearses. They wore these black robes like an army of grim reapers, and they never fucking spoke to anybody. They swooped in after every poor stiff hit the sidewalk, scraped him off the pavement with snow shovels, and piled him in with all the others. What the hell was I supposed to think? Were they government? A cult? Whatever it was, they were organized and so damn weird nobody could even look them in the eye.

"Somehow, through all of this shit, I kept myself reasonably sane. I found a deserted health club and spent most of my time in it. I worked out, swam in the pool, showered in the locker room. I slept on a pile of yoga mats and ate a lot of canned soup. It got harder and harder for me to go outside, especially at night. When it got dark, people got weird, and that was when most of the suicides happened. Right around two, three in the morning. You couldn't walk under tall buildings anymore because someone might come hurtling down on you, screaming or shouting or so quiet you'd think they were only a bad vision until they smacked the sidewalk, splattering blood all over you.

"After a long period when I didn't come out of the health club at all, maybe three or four weeks, I took a walk around the city. At first I thought I was the last person on earth. After all the insane shit I had seen, it was actually sort of relaxing. No one left to coax down from a ledge or take a knife away from. I was alone, and that was cool with me. I was going to walk the entire North American continent. I was going to see all the places I had never seen before, grow old in a well-supplied cabin somewhere, and die a perfectly natural death with no one around to get all worked up over me.

"Of course, I wasn't the last person alive. Not by a long shot. It was hard to tell how many had survived the Despair, since you usually met with them in groups of one, two, maybe three, but I suppose there were something like twenty thousand people still living in K.C. These folks were all different sorts, as far as I could see, but the one thing they had in common was this look that was stunned and depressed at the same time.

"Wild dogs started making appearances in Kansas City. I suppose they sensed how much easy food could be found in the city, including people food. One day I saw a Doberman sprinting through a downtown street with a screaming infant hanging from its jaws like a pink rabbit. I tracked the Doberman through the city and finally killed it, but the baby was hurt real bad. Its round, little tummy was ripped open, and there were little, tiny coils of intestines leaking out of it, already covered with ants and dirt. The baby's eyes were still open and it was screaming, God, how that poor baby boy screamed, and as I looked from the rock in my hand to the baby lying helpless on the ground, I knew what hell was. Hell was having to do something like this."

The Mayor faded off for a moment. Someone in the group coughed. Zero picked up a twig and tossed it into the fire.

"But I did it. I smashed that baby's skull like it was made of eggshell, and there I was, standing over a silent, tiny corpse and a bigger, uglier dog corpse in the middle of what had once been a major American city, with its own laws and cops and shining public fountains. A bad feeling, standing there like that. Like I'd been scraped out, hollowed of everything a human being is supposed to feel.

"I could have killed myself then. I really could have. But I guess I'm too ornery, or thickheaded, and I decided to fight back against the hollow feeling. I broke into a gun store, carried out all the weapons and ammunition I could find, and began rounding up anyone who wanted to help me. I was surprised to find how many people, folks who had been bank tellers, shop clerks, waitresses, bus drivers, you name it, how many different types of people wanted to help me hunt the damn dogs down. I suppose they were tired of sitting on their hands, glad to have something productive to do.

"Slowly I learned to do what I could without exhausting myself, without trying to do too much on my own. I let others help me out. I delegated, like we were all on one big construction crew rebuilding Kansas City. People kept gathering around me, even after we had the worst of attacks under control, and I suddenly found myself the unofficial mayor of Kansas City. You know, I still think I was elected because I look solid and square, like a brick. People really love brick. They just do."

The Mayor sat back from the fire. Orange light flickered across his chiseled face, but his eyes remained fixed on Norman.

"Nothing about the Despair has been pretty, Norman. None of us have come out of it smelling like angels. What matters now is what we do with the time left. That's all. That's all we can do."

12

Everyone stayed up late drinking around the campfire, swapping memories of happier times and toasting to the Last Ten Percent. Norman woke to a warm, cloudless day and the Mayor cooking pancakes over a new, slightly smaller campfire. The big man worked alone, a hefty iron griddle steaming before him as cakes the circumference of softballs turned golden brown. Already a massive stack of pancakes sat beside the griddle, enough for at least five people, and beside the stack was a large glass jar filled with an amber-colored liquid.

The Mayor nodded at Norman as he stumbled to the circle of log seats surrounding the fire. "Morning."

The Mayor shoved a paper plate into Norman's hands. It was stacked with pancakes, but before Norman could count how many exactly, the Mayor was pouring the amber liquid and burying the pancakes from view. "Don't forget syrup," the Mayor ordered. "I tapped it myself."

"Thanks," Norman said, still sleepy enough to not be surprised that a man who had held a gun to his head the day before was now serving him breakfast. He tore a piece of
pancake off and stuffed it into his mouth. Syrup dripped
down his chin. "Thish is the greatish thing I've ever eaten,"
Norman said, meaning it. The Mayor laughed and flipped
another pancake. Zero and Pops entered the clearing and got
some pancakes for themselves. They sat down near Norman
and started to eat.

"Well," the Mayor said, his forehead creasing, "things are
looking better than they used to, that's for sure. People have
come from all over the Midwest to live in Kansas City. We've
taken a residential section of the old city and turned it into a
cozy town all itself. Most of our time is spent collecting food,
making repairs to houses, things like that. I guess we're doing
pretty good, considering we've still got black robes running
around, stealing our dead."

The Mayor smiled and heaped pancakes onto Pops' plate.

Norman swallowed. "Seems too convenient how the Collectors showed up right when the Despair began, doesn't it?"

"We should shoot them all," Zero said. "Shoot them all
and stop the Despair."

Pops and Norman turned to the girl.

Zero tucked a strand of hair behind her ear. "We could,
couldn't we?"

The Mayor rattled the skillet over the fire pit. "Well, I
don't think the Despair is anything you can shoot."

Zero squinted. "What do you mean?"

"I mean even if you walked right up to it, stared into its face, there'd be no way to attack it at all. I don't think the Despair is a material thing at all."

"Then what is it?"

"Could be a ghost, maybe, or something like a ghost. Think of all the people who have died on this planet during the past millions of years. Think of all the tortured souls who could, hypothetically, be walking the face of the planet. There's a lot of them, aren't there? The massacred, the bombed, the hung. The tortured. The diseased and beheaded. You add all those poor souls up and you have a lot of negative energy. Well, maybe all that negative energy has found a place to come together, to unify in its desire for revenge on the living, breathing people who still enjoy a world they no longer have any access to? I'd imagine they'd act upon the living much the same way as this Despair has. They'd suck all the life out of the world, greedy for its warmth, and they'd laugh as remaining husks killed themselves one by one, until the entire world was dead, together again at last."

Pops tossed his paper plate into the fire. "That's an unsettling idea, Mayor."

The Mayor nodded, flipping more pancakes. "Well, the world's become an unsettling place. We may have brought some type of order to Kansas City, but dozens of folks still pass every day by their own hand, despite all our safety checks. The days of living solitary are coming to an end, one way or another."

"We agree," Pops said. "That's why we headed for Seattle

in the first place. We had a drifter come down about a year ago and tell us about a scientist there named Dr. Briggs. Drifter said Briggs was working on a cure for the Despair."

"Ah," the Mayor said. "You've had drifters all the way down to Florida? I wondered how far they'd made it. Drifters love to tell tall tales, seems to me."

"They could be telling the truth," Norman said. "Seattle may be close to a cure."

"I hope he does have a cure," the Mayor said. "Still, it might be safer for you folks to come back with us for a year or two, until we get some sort of proof. We can always use more help with managing the city."

Norman coughed up some pancake. "Thanks for the offer, Mayor, but the Collectors are still looking for me. I don't want to stir up a war when your little city is starting to thrive. Pops and Zero could join you, though. What do you think, guys?"

Pops scratched the silver stubble on his jaw. He'd grown tanner over the past week of outdoor living, and the silver of his thin beard was a sharp contrast with the brown of his skin.

"No thanks, Mr. Mayor," Pops said. "I'd like to see this thing through with Norman. We've been neighbors for a long time, you know. We wrestled alligators together back in Florida."

The big man laughed and tossed a pancake into his mouth as if it were a potato chip. "And what about you, young lady? How do the bright lights of Kansas City sound instead of traveling around with these two old men?"

Zero threw her own plate into the fire and rubbed her hands together. "Thanks, but I've lived in Kansas my whole life. I want to see the ocean."

The Mayor folded his arms across his chest and looked toward the western horizon. "I think you folks are going to see a lot of things. I just hope you live through them."

Norman, Pops, and Zero rocketed through the remainder of Kansas at a reckless forty-eight miles per hour. Pops grinned as he evaded potholes and random debris with the truck, and the flat horizon rolled on. Norman sat back and enjoyed the sun on his face, slipping in and out of sleep as Zero and Pops chatted about U.S. history. The precocious girl was more interested in history than Norman remembered most kids being (probably the result of being cooped up inside her house for five years with only her bookworm dad and a few eccentric neighbors for company). Norman guessed Zero was also a fan of opera music, algebra, and Jane Austen novels. Which was all right, but still a little weird for an eleven-year-old who, in a world only five years gone, might solely have been worried about cute boys, soccer, and shopping. Hell, Zero was probably more cultured than Norman was. He had no interest in books and could barely add his own golf scores anymore. All he had ever wanted to do in life was make a little money, love his wife, and live as comfortably as possible. Even the idea of living outside Florida had left him cold. Why search for paradise when you woke up in it every day?

They crossed the Kansas state line by midmorning. Colorado, at least the first bit of it, was pretty flat. When they reached a town called Burlington, Pops steered them off the interstate and headed north on 385. They'd decided to avoid Denver, and Colorado in general, and take 385 to Interstate 80, then head west, across Wyoming and the northeast corner of Utah.

The roads, all Duracrete, were in amazing shape, and when they rolled through Cheyenne at dusk they hadn't encountered trouble all day. Wyoming's population had been sparse to begin with, and the Despair had likely hit it harder than the more populated areas of the country. This was the final sweeping stretch of prairie before you started to climb upward, before you hit that jagged, snowcapped Rocky Mountain ridge that stretched from northern Canada all the way into the middle of New Mexico. This was big plains country, and when all your friends and family offed themselves, there wasn't much else around for comfort but a lot of open prairie. Around here a lot of clammy, skeletal things could climb into your bed, wrap their cold feelers around your chest, and squeeze, squeeze, squeeze.

That night they camped a few miles outside Cheyenne beside a clear, dark river. The crickets sang for each other as wind gusted down from the west, tousling the wildflowers and high grass.

Norman slept well.

The place suited him.

PART THREE

Highland

13

Jordan loved mountains the way many Midwesterners loved the ocean. Norman could remember driving along the East Coast long before the Despair and hearing her ooh and aah over little dips in the terrain, slight changes he wouldn't have noticed if he had been driving alone. They had driven from Vermont to the Adirondack Mountains as part of their honeymoon, and the farther they drove along the mountain range the more Jordan seemed to return to a happy, childlike state in which everything she saw was so wondrous that she felt the need to point it out to Norman, as if he were incapable of seeing the mountains on his own.

One afternoon Jordan directed Norman to pull off the interstate and take a small gravel road up into the green hills. It was a warm, late September day and the constant chirping of crickets poured in through their open windows—*eeep eeep eeep eeep eeep*—reminding Norman of a small child racked with hiccups. They spotted deer and fox running through the thick undergrowth. Jordan shouted as she pointed the animals out, almost causing Norman to veer off the winding road each time. The high altitude made them high, and by the time Norman pulled off at a "scenic view opportunity," they both giggled easily, at nothing at all. As Norman engaged the car's parking brake, he readied himself for some serious fooling around, yet before he could un-buckle his seat belt Jordan had bolted from the car and scampered toward the edge of the lookout point. Laughing, he followed her.

The lookout point revealed a cozy green view that went on for miles, revealing a good chunk of Virginia and stopping only at a bank of clouds in the distant horizon.

"We can see so far," Jordan said. "Like birds."

Norman stood behind his new wife, hugging her warm body against his. "Reminds me of Ireland. See any lep-rechauns?"

"Not yet. But we haven't been here that long."

Jordan sighed, and Norman could feel her breasts push gently against his arms.

"You know what, Norman? I think we'll be together until we're really old, with gray hair and arthritis and heaps of pills on our night table. We'll drink iced tea in the afternoon and talk about nothing while we watch our great-grandchildren play hide-and-go-seek in the yard. There won't be any wars to read about in the paper by then, so you'll have to read the comics twice and maybe the business section to pass the time.

"Maybe in a hundred years we'll be like these old mountains, tired but satisfied. What do you think of that?"

Norman nuzzled Jordan's neck and hugged his young wife tighter. He planted his feet firmly, the strongest man in the world.

They could see so far.

The road remained passable and they drove deeper across southern Wyoming. Mountains appeared in the distance as hazy clumps of red. The Laramie and Medicine Bow mountains, Zero explained. She'd discovered an ancient road map crammed under the truck's front seat and had been reading it all day, mostly aloud, with her bare feet propped up on the dashboard. She lectured using a singsong voice of mock scholarship that made Norman and Pops grin.

"Gentlemen, we are about to enter the majestic Great Divide Basin. The majestic Great Divide Basin is known all through Wyoming, of course, for its majestic divisionness. In the olden days of yore people came from wide and far to see this local treasure. Families would pile into their vans, campers, SUVs, convertibles, and what have you, driving for hundreds, no, thousands of miles to see this tremendous basin, take a picture, and then look for an overpriced restaurant to eat at. Restaurants, you see, were places where people cooked hot food for you and you paid them with what was called a credit card."

Pops scratched his chin. "Hey, I remember restaurants. Wonderful inventions. You could just go in, sit down, and order anything you felt like right off a menu. Do you remember grilled burgers, Norman? With all the fixings? A pretty little thing bringing the food right to your table, all smiles and 'Have a good meal'? And french fries!"

"Oh, yeah. Restaurants were great."

"Gentlemen, gentlemen," Zero scolded. "We are allowing ourselves to become distracted from this venerable Great Divide Basin. And if we fail to appreciate such a treasure, what's next? Sunsets? Full moons?"

"Well," Pops said as they coasted down the last in a series of hills, "we better shut up and appreciate it then."

The basin was a vast expanse of red rock, scrub brush, and bleached white sky. Norman was reminded of Mars, of the images collected and sent back to Earth by the small scientific settlement there. What had happened to the settlers? Had they heard of the Despair, or were they still now blissfully unaware of the extent of its damage, thinking only that they had lost communication with Earth and that when they finally returned home in a few more years, they would find everything still up and running, their friends and family still alive and a hero's welcome waiting for them?

"Norman, look!"

Zero pointed out the passenger window. A herd of horses had gathered at the edge of the interstate to feed on the wildflowers that grew along the road. Each horse appeared quick and lean, as if it had been wild its entire life. Their red-and-white patchwork coats blended well with the arid terrain, like camouflage.

"Horses," Zero said. "Look at all those horses."

"No dogs are going to catch up with that lot," Pops said. "No, sir."

The herd glanced up at the sound of the truck. It spooked them and they ran off a few hundred yards from the highway, then arced back around in one fluid motion. They stood in an unblinking group as the truck went by. Zero turned to watch them and reported that the herd was cautiously returning to the ditches to sniff the wildflowers and eat weeds.

"Wild," Pops said, nodding at the road ahead. "It's been that long already."

Norman pulled off the interstate early in the afternoon. He could have parked the truck in the middle of the interstate without causing any trouble, but he took a proper exit instead, driving slowly down a cracked road past abandoned gas stations and fast-food restaurants. He pulled off the road and drove up a gently sloping hill. He parked at the hill's crest. "Thought we could have a good view," he said, "you know, for lunch."

They sat on the truck's hood while they ate, absorbing the warm sunlight and the view west. The sky appeared so high and so rolling, it made the red earth below it seem trivial, small enough to be the set of some Hollywood movie, not the next stretch of Wyoming. Norman chewed his ration of dried meat and fruit slowly, giving the food time to grow wet and expand in his mouth. He noticed a small house sitting at the bottom of the hill, covered in feathers.

"Hey, guys, look at that. At the bottom of the hill."

Pops and Zero squinted at the house.

"Weird."

"Covered in something, isn't it? Towels?"

"Looks like feathers," Norman said. "You want to go check it out? Stretch our legs?"

"You two go," Pops said. "Maybe I'll take a little nap."

The descent was steep, and after falling twice, Norman slid down the hill on his backside. Zero rolled most of the way in somersaults, giggling as she sped by Norman. She landed at the bottom of the hill and lay on her back, laughing and pulling bits of grass out of her hair, and Norman remembered that this was how eleven-year-olds were supposed to be. How they used to be.

"How fast you think you were going, there?" Norman asked as he slid to the hill's base and got to his feet. "Hundred miles an hour?"

He gave Zero a hand and pulled her to her feet.

"At least. Maybe two hundred miles per hour."

"That's a good hill, isn't it?"

"The best."

They approached the house covered in feathers and saw it wasn't really covered in feathers at all, but paper. Sheet after sheet of paper. Each piece was nailed to the house like a collection of religious tracts, or shingles. The paper sheets flapped with the breeze so that the house appeared to be breathing.

"Holy cow," Zero said. "Somebody's been busy."

Norman stepped closer to the house. She was right. Someone had written on each sheet of paper not by hand, or computer, but with an old-fashioned typewriter. Norman grasped a sheet at random and read.

```
Today I went outside but nobody felt like
    talking. I didn't feel like talking much,
    either, so I walked around looking for
    lizards or anything else interesting.
    Sunny. Beautiful weather.
```

Norman grabbed another sheet.

```
Willie Nelson wrote a song once about a
    land that knows no parting. I hope he was
    right. I hope a place like that really
    exists.
```

Norman dropped the sheet. Zero was reading the lowest row of papers around the house's foundation. "They keep talking about their parents and their brother and their sister," Zero said, glancing back at Norman. "It's so sad." Norman walked around to the back of the house. The windows had all been boarded up and sheets of paper had been nailed into the boards, too.

```
You think you can beat it. That if you
    ignore it long enough, it'll go away.
    Take the pills. Bask under the sunlamp
```

Exercise. Think "positive." You think
you can outlive the cool, clammy touch
of the Collectors, that YOU'LL never be
collected.

Now, we know better. What happened was far
   worse than your standard depression.
   Perhaps a viral contagion of some sort,
   released by one lone madman? We all have
   our own theories. We all have our losses.
   Now we know better than to wish it all
   away, to cover our eyes and try to dupe
   our bodies with medication. The Despair
   was no fluke, no case of mass hysteria.

The Despair is a howling void. And tonight,
   that void is so easy to feel.

Norman stepped away from the house. The occupant had
also papered the entire roof. He or she had written all this,
climbed up a ladder, and hammered each sheet into place.
The person must have worked feverishly. Dementedly. And,
judging by the reasonably intact condition of the papers, the
person must have done it recently.

Maybe he or she was still alive. Still typing.

Norman went around to the front of the house. The entire
front porch was papered with the exception of the front
door. A white envelope had been nailed to the door, directly

at eye level. When Norman knocked, the door rattled but did not give way.

"Hello?"

No one answered the door. Zero came round from the back and stopped at the edge of the porch stairs.

"What are you doing?"

"Checking to see if they're home."

"You think they will be?"

Norman knocked again. He didn't want to take the letter off the door, and he didn't want to go inside. So he'd stand there, knocking. Someone would come. Someone would answer the door.

"I don't know, Norman. You should read some of that stuff. You read some, didn't you?"

Norman knocked a third time. His breathing was heavy.

"It's a suicide letter, isn't it?"

Someone had written on the outside of the envelope. The handwriting was sloppy. Uneven.

For You

"The whole thing," Zero said. "The whole house. It's one big suicide letter."

The envelope slid off the nail easily enough. He turned it in his hands. Light. Only one or two sheets of paper, max.

"Well, are you going to open it?"

"Should I?"

"Why not?"

His thumb slid easily enough under the envelope's back crease and tore at his touch. He took out the letter and unfolded it in his hands.

```
This house is empty now.
All the houses in all the world are empty
   now.
Thanks for stopping by.
```

Norman held the note up to the sun. White light seared right through it and he winced at the glare.

"What's it say, Norman?"

The girl waited for him to answer with a hand cupped over her forehead, shielding her eyes from the sunlight. Her forehead had wrinkled above her nose, like someone expecting bad news on top of bad news.

"Says, 'Thanks for stopping by,'" Norman said, crumpling the note and throwing it over his shoulder. "How the hell do you like that?"

"Weird. Should we go inside? See if there's anything to nab and take with us?"

"No. We've got everything we need already. No use stirring up dust."

He must have said the right thing, because Zero nodded and began skipping back up the hill, her dark hair swishing against her back. Norman followed the girl at a slower pace. The papered house crackled behind him, almost a sigh.

14

Three days later they stood at the foamy edge of the Great Salt Lake, arms at their sides as they smiled like idiots. Sunlight shimmered off the lake as hundreds of seagulls and pelicans flew overhead, splashing down occasionally to dip their beaks into the red-brown streaks that floated on the lake's surface. Norman was amazed at how big the lake really was. It was no Atlantic Ocean, but it was big. If he closed his eyes and listened to the crashing waves, he could almost imagine that he was back in Florida, walking one smooth stretch of beach after another.

"It's so pretty," Zero said, scanning the lake with an ancient pair of binoculars she'd brought from the truck's cab. They had pulled off the interstate and driven down a flat, unpaved road to the northern edge of the lake. A small, dusty ridge of mountains sat on their right, to the west. To their left was nothing but flat, bleached terrain as far as they could see.

All the birds staggered in midair as an updraft swept

across the lake. "Smells bad," Zero said, crinkling her nose. "Like my dad's whiskey farts."

"Rotten eggs," Pops said. "A lot of saltwater seas smell like this. Something about the drying remains of sea creatures, or some such. Not exactly as beautiful as the beaches back in Florida."

"Well, Zero," Norman said, watching as a pelican scooped something out of the lake and swallowed it whole, "is the Great Salt Lake as cool as you thought it'd be?"

Zero smiled. "It's great, even with the smell. Thanks for stopping."

Norman reached down and picked up a handful of sand. "Must be a ton of minerals in the water. I bet if we threw you in, Zero, you'd float like a boat."

"Don't really want to swim in something that smells so bad, but thanks."

"You sure?"

"Oh, yeah. I'm sure."

The natural beach stretched a long way. They walked in a scattered way, searching the sand for seashells and other washed-up treasure. Norman found a wedding ring missing its diamond, and Pops found a shoe (both items possibly cast-off refuse from the suicides that had once littered the southeast edge of the lake, the side bordering Salt Lake City. In the early days of the Despair, there'd been footage of massive body logjams across Salt Lake, or "corpse rafts").

The sun began to descend as they combed the beach. When Norman snapped out of his beachcomber's trance, he was surprised how close they'd come to the low mountain range to the west. Less than half a mile, as the seagull flew. He called to Pops and Zero and they gathered around a slime-covered piece of driftwood.

"We should probably head back, don't you think?"

"Sure," Pops said. "I'm getting sore from the pigeon-toed way you have to walk on all this sand."

"Zero?"

The girl wiped her hands on the front of her jeans. "Yeah, we can go. But I haven't found anything cool yet."

"Maybe on the way back."

They turned around. The sun was at their back now, and Norman didn't have to squint anymore.

"Hey," Norman said, halting. "Let me see those binoculars, Zero."

She handed them over. He brought the binoculars up and adjusted the focus. Their truck, far down the beach, now had company. Five men on horseback had surrounded it and were circling it uneasily, as if worried it had been booby-trapped. What did the horsemen have strapped to their backs?

"Oh," Norman said. "More crazies."

Pops and Zero stopped walking.

"What?"

"Around the truck. Five men, on horseback. Looks like they're all armed, too. With . . . swords?"

"No way."

"Christ."

One of the riders broke from the circle and started toward the beach. The other riders also broke off and followed the first rider. They were following a trail in the sand. Their trail.

"Coming towards us," Norman said. "Any thoughts?"

"Could be friendly," Zero said. "Maybe they just want to talk, like the Mayor."

Norman winced. The riders were moving fast, their horses kicking up thick clouds of sand. Ten minutes away? Five?

"They have swords, honey. Swords and horses. What are the odds they're normal, well-adjusted folks?"

"Screw it," Pops said. "Let's head for the hills. Retreat."

"Into the mountain range?"

"Only decent cover I can see," Pops said. "Unless you feel like a real long, salty swim."

"The hills it is," Norman said. "We better hustle, too."

They found a narrow pass through the hills and hiked until the lake, and the riders, were out of sight. Another emergency council was held, and they decided that, despite having no food, weapons, or bedding, they should hike farther into the hills so they could find a good spot to hide and let the horseback riders, if they were still in pursuit, pass them by. So they hiked farther, up a steady incline, until they met the crying boy.

The little boy sat on a rock right off the path, dressed in a white kimono. His knees were pulled up to his chest, his head buried in his arms. Norman took a few tentative steps toward the boy, wondering if he was real or if this was the mountain's resident ghost. Norman wiped his hands on the front of his jeans.

"Hello?"

The boy glanced up but showed no surprise at seeing strangers on the mountain path. Tears trickled down the boy's smooth, olive-colored cheeks and left half-dried traces of water.

"Don't worry, we won't hurt you." Norman turned back to Pops and Zero. "What should I do?"

"Talk to him," Zero said. "Duh."

Norman knelt in front of the boy but kept a small distance. "My name is Norman. What's your name?"

"Angelo," the boy whispered, so soft Norman could barely hear him. Then the boy's head dropped and he full-out wept, his small chest hitching as he sucked down air. Zero stepped forward and put her arm around the little boy's shoulder. The boy wept a while longer, but eventually his breathing slowed and he wiped his eyes with the sleeve of his white kimono. Zero patted the boy gently on the back. He leaned toward the girl and whispered into her ear. Norman rubbed his hands and wondered if he was hearing the sound of galloping horses nearby.

"You know, we don't have a ton of time here for random consolation."

"It's his grandpa, I think. He's sad about his grandpa."

Pops knelt in front of the boy, the oily knee of his overalls brushing against the white silk of the boy's kimono. "It's okay, little guy. Are you lost? Did you lose your grandpa?"

Angelo nodded, eyes on the ground.

Pops grinned and tousled the boy's hair. "Don't worry, son. If he's around here, we'll find him."

The boy shook his head yes but did not smile. When they started up the path again, he came along with them, holding Zero's hand as if she were his newfound babysitter. "Good God," Norman said. "We might as well be a parade now."

Pops laughed. "Just need the marching band, right? Gooooooo, Gators!"

They came to the mountain's summit. Below them sat a flat, rocky plain. Norman scanned the horizon with the binoculars, and sure enough, a large encampment was parked right below them on the edge of the range. Dozens of tents, big and small, all of them swarmed with riders on horseback. Well, maybe it was only the last performing American circus.

"Is that where you live, Angelo?" Norman asked. "Do you live in that camp down there, the one with all the horses?"

The boy nodded.

"That's great," Norman said, starting down the path toward the camp. "I'm sure your grandfather will be happy to see you. Have a good hike back home, okay?"

The boy burst into tears. Zero and Pops scowled at Norman, who threw his hands into the air.

"What? You really think we should go down there?"

"We can't let him walk down alone," Zero said. "What if he falls and breaks his neck?"

"That's not a bad way to die—"

"Norman," Pops said. "We better do this one, too. You know how fortune turns. We can use all the good luck we can get."

"But, Pops—"

The boy wailed louder at Norman's shouting. Zero bent over the boy, cooing to him. Pops clucked his tongue against the roof of his mouth.

Norman ran his hands through his hair. "Okay, fine. Let's take him back home, if you two are such Good Samaritans. Hope they're not cannibals."

Zero hoisted Angelo into her arms. "It's okay, Angelo. We know you're not a cannibal. Norman's a little paranoid, that's all."

Pops laughed and patted Norman on the back. "Everything will be fine, Norman. Don't worry."

Angelo's grandfather had not spoken since their arrival in his tent. The old man's hair was wet, as if he had recently bathed, and like his grandson, he was also dressed in a white kimono. His skin was a darker, more wrinkled version of Angelo's olive complexion, but it was easy to see the family resemblance in the clear, brown eyes. Angelo's grandfather sat with his hands folded on the desk, considering both—Norman and Pops—with an unflinching gaze, and Norman couldn't decide if they were in trouble or sitting with a new friend. Zero had already gone off with a group of women at little Angelo's insistence, and now two stony-faced guards were posted at the tent's entrance, each improbably armed with samurai swords.

Norman leaned forward. "Sir? Do you know what's happened to our friend? She went off with some wo—"

"My name is Fernando del Cardenio," their host interrupted. "Who are you?"

Pops extended a hand, which Cardenio ignored. "My name is Franklin Conway, sir, but you can call me Pops."

Cardenio turned to Norman. "And you?"

Norman ran a hand through his hair. "Name's Steve Farmer. We found your grandson crying in the hills and decided to bring him back home. We're not looking for a reward or anything. Just want to get back on the road. You know. Keep on trucking."

Cardenio grunted. "The boy is taking all this rather hard. He should be joyful at my Passing, but he is still young. He fails to see the larger picture." Cardenio waved a hand at the tent around them. "He doesn't see that beyond this world is another, greater world, of which we must strive to obtain access through prayer, service, and reverence to the Almighty Source, Keeper of Heaven and Hell. Young Angelo does not heed the call of the stars yet. He does not understand these times of Despair. Angelo sees only his grandfather, the only surviving member of his family, and weeps at losing him."

Cardenio clasped his hands and shut his eyes. Norman

glared at Pops. He'd been right all along. Another crazy. Another goddamn crazy bastard, and now they found themselves trapped inside this creepy circus tent, at the random mercy of a stranger's insanity.

"And what about you, gentlemen?" Cardenio said, waking from his reverie. "Do you believe the Collectors, as servants of the Source, are culling humanity for a greater purpose?"

Pops cleared his throat and pushed his glasses up the bridge of his nose. "Well, sir, I reckon there is a God, but beyond that I really couldn't say. When my wife died, I stopped trying to figure out all the details and settled for living the life I saw around me. If there is a heaven, I'm sure my wife will be there, along with all the other poor souls taken by the Despair, and hopefully I'll end up there someday myself. Though, after the last few years, I wouldn't be surprised if I went the other way, either."

Cardenio blew on his clean, manicured fingernails. "What about you, Mr. Farmer? What do you believe?"

Norman recalled staying up late with Jordan in college, discussing big questions like this during rambling, moonlit strolls around campus. They'd walked hand in hand, their feet crunching on soft grass and twigs as they passed sleeping administration buildings, throbbing dorms, and into the darker, more densely wooded edges of campus as philosophic generalities flowed between them, the evening stars growing increasingly bright above their heads. Big, optimistic ideas had come easily back then, yet most of what they believed and thought had now been relegated to so much naïve gibberish by the Despair. No more moonlit walks for them, no more discussions.

"I don't think there's anything after death," Norman said, staring straight at Cardenio. "It's all darkness. It's like sleeping, but without dreams and you never wake up. I suppose the ghost of a person sometimes remains behind, a sort of energy resonance of the soul. But other than that, death is lights out and good night."

Cardenio bent over in his chair. He closed his eyes, clasped his hands, and mumbled an unintelligible prayer. When he finished praying, he sat up again and crossed his arms.

"How can you continue to live while believing such things, Mr. Farmer? Why weren't you the first to die, in the early days of the Despair?"

Norman scratched his head. "Don't know, I guess. I was in love back then. I had a wife."

"Many people had others. Many people were in love. Are you trying to say your love for her was better than all these other loves? That it provided you nourishment while others starved?"

"No. I wouldn't say that."

"Then what would you say? What answer would you give me?"

Norman smirked. "I guess I'm not going to give anyone the satisfaction of saying, 'Better you than me,' until I absolutely have to. Actually, I wouldn't mind being the last breathing person on the face of this earth."

Cardenio chuckled softly. "If it is stubbornness that's brought you this far, Mr. Farmer, you must be one stubborn son of a bitch."

Everyone laughed at this, and for a second the interview wasn't strange at all, more like three grad students discussing philosophy in a bar.

Then Cardenio stopped smiling. "Laughter aside, gentlemen, I see it is Fate that has brought you here. You are not considered prisoners, yet, but as the head of this clan, I cannot allow you to leave us with such dreadful sins etched upon your hearts. Luckily, you have arrived at our little camp on a most auspicious night. The moon is full, and I have been selected to Pass into Eternity by the holy stars themselves. I will make sure you both have good seats this evening, and I would not be surprised to find that your views on death have quite changed by the morning's light. I must go and meditate now, but I shall see you both soon at my Farewell Dinner."

Norman grinned and rubbed his hands together. "You're kidding us about this whole Passing thing, right? Just a small joke on the new guys, something to scare us straight?"

"No," Cardenio said. "Some things we do not joke about."

A guard stepped out from behind a silk screen Norman hadn't noticed. Cardenio smiled, his dark eyes glittering as if they'd been stuffed with broken glass. "Make sure these gentlemen bathe, please," he said. "They are unclean."

15

After bathing, Norman and Pops found their clothes missing and carefully folded, immaculate blue kimonos in their place. Their guard explained that their clothes were now being "purified," which Norman hoped wasn't another way of saying "burnt to a pile of ashes."

Little Angelo appeared in the opening of their small tent. "You look better now. Clean."

Pops gave Angelo a deep bow. "Thank you. I feel clean, probably for the first time in months."

Angelo returned the bow. "Please follow me, Mr. Pops and Mr. Farmer. It's time for dinner."

They followed Angelo outside. The sun had dipped below the horizon, turning the sandy ground a strange Mars red. All the tents they passed were empty, and nothing moved through the campground except them. Angelo led them back to Cardenio's tent, which was by far the largest in camp. Zero waited for them at the entrance, spotlessly clean and dressed in an emerald green kimono. Her hair had been braided and pulled back, revealing her high cheekbones. "Aren't these people great?" Zero said, beaming. "They let me take a bath, gave me this pretty kimono, and even braided my hair!"

Norman shook his head. "Didn't they tell you what was happening tonight?"

"What do you mean?"

A burly man in a black kimono emerged from Cardenio's tent and gestured at them to enter. Murmuring voices and clattering dishes could be heard behind him, the subdued rattle of a dinner party.

"Hurry," Angelo said, grabbing Zero's hand and tugging her toward the tent. "They're going to start soon."

Zero and Angelo entered the tent first, followed by Norman and Pops. The tent was much different from the dim, musty place they had entered earlier that afternoon. It was now illuminated by four iron candelabra, their numerous candles filling the room with a soft yellow light that caused the hanging tapestries around them to glow, revealing woven images of golden dragons, flying cranes, bamboo stalks, and rolling mountainsides. A long table had been placed in the middle of the tent, at which three dozen people sat in metal folding chairs. Cardenio was seated to the far right of the table, with everyone else in the room on his left. Angelo ushered Norman, Pops, and Zero to their seats on the far left of the table.

Norman sat down and scanned the various faces in the room. All ages, all skin colors, and all dressed in colorful kimonos. They did not look exceptionally fierce, or blood-thirsty. In fact they seemed like everyone else Norman had encountered during the Despair. They had the same hunched posture, the same bleary eyes, the same general air of loss. Weird to see so many people sitting in the same room. Did Seattle feel like this, only bigger?

The food was brought out, and no one spoke as the group ate. Norman drank rice wine from a porcelain thimble and rummaged through the pile of steamed seaweed on his plate, poking awkwardly into the mass with his chopsticks. He stole glances at the open tent flap, hoping to see a steaming platter with some meat on it, or at least some mashed pota-toes, but no other courses came forward. When everyone had finished his or her "meal," a man sitting in the middle of the table stood up. He was wearing a long sword over his shoul-der and a short sword in the belt of his black robe, and his dark face was deeply lined. "Fernando del Cardenio," the man said, "I, Timothy Lee Jones, would like to announce that the preparations are now in order for your Passing. I will be your assistant tonight in this glorious endeavor and would now hear any requests you would make of me."

Jones remained standing as Cardenio dabbed his mouth with a silk napkin.

"Thank you, Timothy. You have always been a good friend and an honorable man. May the Collectors bless you and keep you always."

Jones bowed at the praise, his sword shifting against his back.

"As for requests," Cardenio continued, standing up to address the room, "I only ask for little Angelo to be taken care of properly. With my Passing he will no longer have any blood relatives, and he will rely on this clan's generosity until he reaches a more productive age. Yet I am certain, in this magnificent community of Believers, that he will find himself cared for until the Collectors come for him as well."

Jones bowed again and everyone else stood up as well, as if on cue. They clustered around Cardenio and said good-bye to him, hugging him one by one. Norman felt his heart lurch as he noticed Angelo around Cardenio's knees, squeezing his grandfather as if afraid that a strong wind would come along and blow the old man away. Pops and Zero joined Norman on the far opposite side of the tent.

"We need to get the hell out of here," Pops said beneath his breath. "I don't know what's about to happen, but I reckon it's not going to be pleasant."

Zero grabbed Norman's elbow. "What's going on?"

"He's going to kill himself tonight."

"Who?"

"Angelo's grandfather."

"What? He can't do that!"

"Shhhh. Quiet."

"But—"

Norman put an arm around the girl. "Keep cool, okay? We'll get out of here. Don't worry."

"But what about Angelo?"

"You heard the speech. He'll be taken care of."

"By these psychos? Ha."

Norman leaned in and spoke into the girl's ear. "We can't save the whole world. Now, if you want to get out of here in one piece, you're going to have to shut up."

Zero pushed Norman away. "Okay. Whatever."

A woman gave Cardenio a kiss on the cheek and left the tent quickly. Angelo, who was still glued to his grandfather, had to be pried off by two guards as the good-byes concluded. Cardenio looked at the ground as his screaming grandson was carried out of the tent. He gestured for Norman, Pops, and Zero with one hand, his solemn face lit by the flickering candelabra overhead.

"Come along, everyone. Let's see what we shall see."

A full moon had risen, bloated and white. Norman thought the hills east of camp appeared unearthly in the moonlight. Was it possible that the small mountain range was actually a portal to a different world, one with its own beliefs, rituals, and value systems? Or had they stepped into the future, one that was about to sweep away the Last Ten Percent as the Despair continued, unchecked by medicine or rationality or even familial love?

Everyone gathered on a flat stretch of ground beyond the tents, sitting cross-legged on mats and rugs in front of two bright torches. Norman, Pops, and Zero were ushered to one of the front mats by a silent old woman. Behind the torches was another straw mat, where Cardenio sat facing the crowd. Jones, Cardenio's self-professed assistant, came forward into the ring of firelight with a short sword held flat on the palms of his hands. Cardenio bowed and took the sword from his assistant. He unsheathed the sword and held it up, as if to consider its short blade and how it glinted blue with moonlight. Jones stood off to Cardenio's left, slightly behind the sitting man, and Norman saw that the assistant was armed with a long sword of his own.

Cardenio bowed. He slipped his kimono off his shoulders and it dropped to his waist. He tucked the sleeves of his outfit under his knees and pointed the short sword towards his bare stomach. "I offer myself to thee, Collectors, Angels of the Source. Please remove my body from these unclean sands. I am certain we will all meet again in a place filled with Light, Water, and God."

Cardenio bowed deeply once more to the crowd, then plunged the sword into the left side of his stomach. Zero pressed her face into Norman's shoulder as Cardenio slowly drew the dagger across his stomach, his face unflinching, to the right side of his body. At the end of the cut, Cardenio turned the sword and gave it a sharp jerk upward. Someone moaned. Cardenio drew the dagger out of the bloody incision and knelt toward the crowd, extending his neck. Jones stepped forward and swiftly brought his sword down, severing Cardenio's head almost completely, stopping only at the patch of skin covering his throat. Cardenio's head dropped onto his opened chest and dangled by the throat's skin, as if he wished to peer into his own heart, before his entire body collapsed forward into the sand.

Norman glanced around. The crowd was smiling, their faces flushed as if they had all just glimpsed heaven itself. A dark scarlet stain bloomed around the corpse as Jones wiped the blade of his sword with a towel and stepped back. "It is done," the executioner shouted, turning to the north and bowing. "Come for him, sweet angels, and let him rejoin the Source!"

The crowd stood and erupted in applause. As they cheered, their individual voices merged into one continuous, droning hum that made Norman's throat feel dry, as if he hadn't had a drink of fresh water in weeks. He closed his eyes and saw those familiar patches of luminous white lights drifting slowly across his mind, as if they had all the time in the world.

The postsuicide party was festive. A makeshift band had gathered in front of the crowd as Cardenio's body was covered with a white sheet. Two men strummed acoustic guitars, another played the fiddle, and a pretty young woman danced, sang, and beat on a tambourine, twirling before the crowd in a crimson kimono, her eyes flashing like a cat's in the torchlight. The crowd sang along with the band, their heads bobbing up and down as their bodies swayed to the strange, chantlike melody:

For You and Only You, Great Collector
I give this humble offering of my love.
For You are the Source who calls us home,
For You shed the pain of this mortal life,
And ease all our trouble with Death,
Sweet and Pure Death.

Norman didn't see on-duty guards nearby. "Okay," he said. "Time to go, everyone."

"Sure." Pops sounded groggy, as if he were still waking from a nightmare. They wound their way through the crowd, trying not to get noticed. Dusty bottles of red wine were passed about, as well as bowls of fruit and platters of sizzling meat. Norman had to decline food and drink several times as the celebrants grew looser, singing along with the band and groping each other in the sand. Why did death and sex go so well together? Norman could still remember watching the suicide channel with Jordan in the kitchen, somber and sick at heart, and then minutes later they would be making love on the sofa, or on their bed upstairs, moaning as they wrapped their bodies together. Death shouldn't make you feel like having sex, but it did. Was it simply because sex was life-affirming, or was there more to it than that? Perhaps good sex was a way of killing all the bad things that clung to a person, of murdering the invisible demons that threatened to leech away a person's life.

"What's going on now?" Zero asked, her voice small and dazed.

"Ah, I believe this is turning into an orgy," Norman said, looking around for guards on horseback. The mountains weren't too far away now. They could run.

"An orgy?" Zero echoed, stumbling over someone's discarded shoe. "Why are they having an orgy? Mr. Cardenio just killed himself."

"That's why, actually."

"Oh. Sick."

They reached the edge of the crowd. Norman felt a tug on the back of his kimono. He turned slowly, bracing himself for a fight.

It was the boy. Angelo.

"Mr. Farmer, I have your clothes. I saved them from cleansing."

"Thank you, Angelo."

Norman bowed and took the pile of folded clothes. Angelo staggered as the weight was lifted from him, but his eyes remained locked on Norman's.

"My grandfather's dead."

"Yes, Angelo," Norman said, putting a hand on the boy's shoulder. "He is."

"Where has Grandfather gone? Do you think he is with the Source?"

"I don't know much about that, Angelo," Norman said. "I haven't died yet, so I can't really tell you what 'the Source' really means. But I do know that you shouldn't try following him, okay? You shouldn't ever kill yourself like that, no matter what anyone tells you. Do you understand, Angelo?"

"Yes. I understand."

"Good."

In the distance the chanting band stopped playing, and the sound of moaning could be heard clearly now. Angelo didn't seem to notice the noise. The little boy had probably experienced a Passing before and was accustomed to this animal-like behavior.

"You're all leaving, aren't you? You're going away."

Norman squatted down. "Yes. I'm sorry."

"Even Miss Zero?"

"Yes. Even Miss Zero."

Angelo sniffled and wiped his nose. "They always have two guards riding around camp on Passing nights. I will go and distract them. Please give me five minutes before you leave."

Norman took Angelo's hand and shook it. "Thank you, Angelo. You are very brave."

The boy hugged everyone, whispered good-bye, and ran off into the dark. Norman distributed the clothes Angelo had returned to them. They dressed quickly, shedding their kimonos like silken snakeskins. Norman led the way toward the hills and they did not look back.

Though the moon was full, it was still difficult navigating the mountain trail and its sudden, yawning precipices. After they had ascended far enough to be comfortably out of range of any guards, Norman stopped the group at a small clearing in the trail. They dropped to the ground, curled against the rocks, and fell into a cold, shallow sleep. They woke to a murky dawn and the sound of the sky being beaten. "Helicopter," Norman told Zero. "That's what a helicopter sounds like."

They found a scraggly, half-dead tree and sat down beneath it, making themselves as small as possible.

Zero pressed her hands over her ears. "Helicopters sound terrible. Like giant bat wings flapping."

"Oh, they're wonderful machines," Pop said, squinting at the gray sky. "Marvelous fliers."

The thumping noise grew louder until it was right over them. The helicopter was bigger than the one Norman remembered from Florida and looked vaguely military. After the chopper passed them by and disappeared beyond the mountains, heading in the direction of Angelo's camp, they continued forward.

They moved slowly, stopping several times to rest as the sun came out and the day grew hotter, and it was late afternoon by the time they emerged from the hills. Norman squinted into the horizon. The sun was bright and the salted terrain wavered in the heat. Still, he could make out their truck in the distance, a small red dot against the flat expanse. They moved steadily toward it, mirage or not.

16

Idaho was empty. Hot, sandy, and empty. The truck ran well and Interstate 84 was in relatively good shape, all the way through Boise and beyond. They traveled through the sagebrush country without any major incidents, resupplying when they needed to and camping in the truck. No one spoke about the past. Talk centered around food, the weather, and how many miles they covered each day. Seattle loomed larger and larger in their minds, its needle-shaped shadow falling across their minds each morning when they woke up and each night before they fell asleep. The promise of warm beds and hot food. The Cure.

They crossed into Oregon and their long string of good luck began to make Norman uneasy. Spots of darkness flitted across the corner of his vision. His skin went clammy without warning, then warmed until he felt feverish. The wound on his forearm had nearly healed, the self-dissolving stitches long disappeared, but the wound throbbed when exposed to sunlight, as if someone had sewn a bomb under his skin.

And that steady humming sound in the back of his mind.

It was stronger.

They entered the Blue Mountains. Norman drove hunched over the steering wheel, worried that another deer or fallen log would appear around a bend in the road as they climbed. Zero and Pops watched the road with him, hypnotized by the endless trees and winding terrain.

"When we get to Seattle, the first thing I'm going to do is go see the ocean," Zero said abruptly, as if answering a question. "I know the water's cold, but I'd like to have a picnic on the beach. They have beaches there, right?"

"Never been," Pops said, "but sounds like a safe bet to me."

"Do you like to swim, Pops?"

"Sure do."

"What about snorkeling? You like to snorkel?"

Pops grinned. "Sure. Went snorkeling in Honduras once, with my wife."

"Really?"

"Oh, yeah. Heck, I remember snorkeling out past the coral reefs. I was a strong swimmer then, you know, a Florida boy through and through. Water was so damn clear, too, with only a tiny blur around the edge of things. Swam until I reached the shelf of the shoreline, a huge drop-off at least forty feet deep. Swam beyond the drop-off, and it was like skimming along the roof of a whole other world.

"I was pretty far out when I came to this huge blue pillar, sitting in the middle of nowhere. The pillar looked so formed, so *made,* that I thought it was artificial. But as I swam closer, I saw the pillar was actually just coral after all. Gave me the chills, actually. I started thinking about Atlantis and how it was supposed to be a marvelous city island, with very advanced technology and science and things like that, yet it disappeared after some vague disaster. Big as the island was, they say it sank in one single day. Made me think that maybe I was swimming over a chunk of some ancient city, the remains of an entire culture buried under all that sand. The feeling was so strange, so damn unsettling, that I headed back to shore right away."

Pops licked his lips. "I didn't really believe Atlantis was real back then. I didn't think it was possible that such a great civilization could exist, only to disappear from the face of the earth after one big setback. Now, I'm not too sure."

Zero opened her mouth, but didn't speak. She cocked her head toward the truck's open passenger window. Her brown eyes widened.

"Oh, shit," she said. "The bats are coming."

Norman felt the tiny hairs on his arms lift. He pressed the accelerator to the floor and the truck lurched upward.

Pops cleared his throat. "What's that, dear?"

"Helicopters," Zero said, turning around in her seat. "Can't you hear them?"

In the rearview mirror Norman saw a wide shadow skimming toward them. They crested the top of a hill, not going nearly fast enough.

"Sorry, guys," Norman said. "I think our luck's run out."

The explosion lifted the truck off the road, its metal frame shrieking as it slammed against the rocky hillside. The windshield shattered and Norman flew from his seat, his seat belt snapping apart as if it were made of paper. His body soared into the air and the horizon spun around him—earth sky earth sky earth sky—and then he struck something hard and blacked out. When he regained consciousness, he saw a confusing blur of fire and metal all around him, on top of him. He had fallen at the foot of an old, gnarled tree. He felt a sudden urge to crawl under its sinewy roots and hide from the *whump whump whump whump* noise as a helicopter landed nearby, somewhere close. Norman could not think properly, could not remember how this had happened. His legs felt as if they had been severed, but when he sat up, Norman saw he was only pinned down by a piece of wreckage. Pops lay in the middle of the road a few yards away, staring up at the sky.

"Pops! Help me get this off my legs."

Pops did not answer. He was staring at the heavens, as if daydreaming the clouds into animals. Perhaps the old man was thinking about mechanical things, about adjustments he still wanted to make to his modified golf cart back in Florida, alterations that would enable the cart to go sixty, seventy miles per hour. Norman shouted at Pops again, wondering why his friend was wearing such a placid expression on his face after hell had broken out all around them. Then he noticed the bloodstains pooling on Pops' chest.

"Pops? You okay?"

The old man didn't answer. He didn't breathe. Norman howled in the general direction of the helicopter, which had landed higher up the road. He clawed at the smoldering wreckage that pinned his legs until his fingers began to bleed. He thought of murder, of wrapping his hands around some faceless Collector's neck and squeezing until the bastard's eyes popped out.

"Zero? You okay, hon?"

No answer, or at least nothing Norman could hear over the helicopter noise. He was growing cold. Shock was setting in, or else he was dying, too. Perhaps his legs had actually been severed and he was bleeding to death. What a strange feeling—

"You are not dying, Norman."

Norman sat up. A tall figure in a black cloak appeared above him, blocking out the sun. The figure lowered its hood, revealing a woman's pale, gaunt face and gray eyes. The Collector smiled without revealing her teeth and pointed a bony finger at Norman's chest.

"I can hear your heartbeat, Murderer of Thompson. I can hear it beating in your Straggler's chest."

"You came to my house," Norman said, recalling the woman's face. "Here to finish me off, huh?"

The Collector lowered her hand. "No, Norman. You are

not worth murdering. Eventually you will Pass here naturally, pinned to this ancient tree. Soon vultures will circle above you, waiting patiently, and mosquitoes will cover your face. You will know a great thirst and a great hunger, and after a drawn-out period of exposure you will die out here, alone. It will be a death befitting such a treacherous animal.

"But do not worry. We'll come back for you, and in the end you, like everyone else, will finally serve the Source."

"Like that cult in Utah? Like Cardenio?"

The woman shrugged her narrow shoulders. "If they choose to actively accelerate the Collection, that is their business. One must admire their devotion, their strong sense of purpose. Does it surprise you that such a faithful group has sprung up in these glorious times?"

"No," Norman said. "People go crazy all the time."

The Collector smiled again, still not showing her teeth. "Who is to say they are insane? Maybe they are quite sane. Maybe they are the only rational members of humanity left. Why do you struggle so mightily against death? It is as inevitable as night following day. Perhaps it is the few remaining Stragglers who are the truly insane ones. You are like moths trapped behind glass, futilely beating your wings for an escape that will never come."

Norman closed his eyes. He was fading away quickly, as if someone had pulled his plug.

"We did not murder your wife, Norman. Thompson did not murder her. Yet you murdered Thompson, didn't you? You shot him in the head."

"He was trespassing," Norman said, his thoughts thickening. "In our house."

The Collector said something in reply, but Norman had already slipped into a different nightmare.

The last time Norman attended church the Despair had been ravaging the world for three months. He attended a barebones, nondenominational church. It had whitewashed walls and skylights. A podium was set up in the front of the room, and instead of pews people sat in rows of cushioned folding chairs. Two banners were draped on the wall behind the podium. The banners portrayed white, fluffy clouds floating against a crackling blue sky and bright, lemon-colored suns with stitched rays of sunshine exploding in all directions. One banner said PEACE and the other banner said LOVE.

Pops came to the service with Norman. They sat alone in the back of the church (Jordan had opted to stay home and work in their garden, and Helen had already taken her desperate leap from the water tower). As the congregation trickled in, the pastor was nowhere to be seen.

"Everyone's moving like they're underwater," Norman said, watching a woman wrapped in a red shawl shuffle through the door and slowly make her way across the room. She kept her eyes on the floor, her fist clenched tightly on the fabric of her shawl. The church was half-full and Norman was surprised to see even that many people in attendance. God wasn't the most popular figure these days. At least not a happy, sunny God who believed in life. That sort of God was going out of style pretty quick.

"Here he is," Pops said, nodding toward the man passing them in the aisle. Pastor Jake wore a white robe and a large gold cross around his neck. He walked speedily and without glancing at the crowd. Normally the young man had a smile for the whole room and walked slowly, so people could notice him approaching the podium and finish their conversations.

When he reached the podium, Pastor Jake turned and faced the congregation. He was handsome, with sandy blond hair and white teeth, but today Norman thought his eyes were too big. Too glassy.

"I am glad you could make it this Sunday," Pastor Jake began. "As you know, it has been three months since the Tokyo suicides."

The congregation murmured at this. It was easy to forget that one event, on one single day, appeared to have triggered the entire Despair. Easy to forget that there had been a time when your friends, family, and neighbors weren't systematically killing themselves.

"It has been three months," Pastor Jake continued. "Three months and many, many lives lost to this evil sweeping the world. This Despair. And as many of you know, I lost my own wife only two weeks ago."

Norman leaned forward. He hadn't known that, actually. He hadn't been to church for a while.

"My wife's death was very hard on my daughter, as you can all understand." Pastor Jake tried to smile again but his lips folded under, as if they couldn't take the weight. "I've discussed heaven with my daughter. I've discussed where her mommy has gone. But my daughter is only five years old, and she misses her mommy."

Members of the congregation nodded. They knew all too well what Pastor Jake was talking about.

"And what happens when we miss somebody? What do we try to do about it?"

Someone coughed, but no one answered.

"We visit them. We go to see them."

Pastor Jake reached into the folds of his robe and pulled out a small black handgun. Norman stood up. He didn't know where he was going to go, but he stood up anyway.

"This morning I found my little girl on the bottom of our pool. She had filled her pockets with rocks and tied some running weights to her ankles so she'd sink better, so she wouldn't float back up again. I think she learned to sink from her mother, who used a jump rope and a concrete block."

Pastor Jake held up the handgun in front of him. The congregation remained still and seated. Pops tugged at Norman's belt.

"Sit down, son. Let the man have his say."

Norman sat down.

"My friends," Pastor Jake said, his glassy eyes sweeping across the congregation. "My dear, dear friends, it has become blatantly obvious to me, and perhaps to you as well, that our God has abandoned us. I have prayed for guidance and I have heard nothing. I have beseeched the Lord day and night, and an endless parade of death has been the Lord's only response. I can only assume, believing as I do that God is just, that we now live in a world without God."

The crowd murmured. Pastor Jake held up the gun for silence.

"We must all make our own decisions, but I for one have decided not to live in a world without God. A world without God is a world full of jackals, vultures, and Collectors. A world without God is not worth living."

Pastor Jake brought the gun to his head, pressed it against his right temple, and pulled the trigger. The shot echoed off the room's acoustic tiles, stunningly loud. Pastor Jake's body slumped to the floor, half out of sight behind the podium. You could see his feet, though, and Norman winced as they twitched. Still the congregation remained in their seats, as if this were all part of the sermon and Pastor Jake was bound to get up again and continue the service.

He didn't.

Someone began to weep, and this snapped the congregation out of their immobility. Clothes rustled as people began talking. The woman in the red shawl stood up from her seat, slowly walked up to the podium, and examined the pastor's body. "He's dead," she called out. She draped her red shawl over the pastor's body and picked up the handgun. The woman didn't turn to face the congregation, didn't even bother to say any last words, before she also shot herself in the head.

"Hell," Pops said. "Hell hell hell hell . . ."

Others began to stand and collect their belongings. They

spoke to each other in soft voices and shuffled toward the podium. They formed a line.

"Is this really happening?" Norman asked Pops. "Really happening?"

"Oh, boy. I hope not."

A man in a long-sleeved purple shirt stood at the head of the line. He took off his shirt and draped it over the red-shawl woman's body. He pried the gun out of her small, claw-shaped hand and held it to his temple as he stood up. "Good-bye," he said, and shot himself. The tall, blond woman behind him carefully covered the dead man with her sweater, then she shot herself, too. The next person in line stepped forward, then the next, and the next.

Eventually the gun ran out of bullets and a dozen dejected people were left alive, shuffling out the door and into the Sunday afternoon as they searched for another way to die. Norman and Pops were left alone in the church. The front of the church was covered with blood and gore, PEACE and LOVE.

They sat a while longer, thinking things over.

17

Norman woke with a horde of mosquitoes covering his face. He swatted the bloodsuckers away and looked over to the middle of the road where Pops had been lying. The spot was empty. They'd taken the old man's body. And Zero. Where was Zero? He needed to get up. He couldn't.

One of the truck axles, with some undercarriage still attached, pinned him against the gnarled tree. Norman slid his hands under the wreckage and lifted. Thing barely gave at all. Just enough to lift off his legs and slam back down again, sending a healthy jolt of pain through his bones. Norman cursed and fell back against the tree's cluster of exposed roots. The sun had dipped below the Blue Mountains while he'd been unconscious. Night fell quick up here. Quick and cold, and then the nocturnal creatures came out to play.

"Okay," Norman said aloud. "What the hell would Pops say about this?"

Pops, Pops, Pops.

The mechanical genius.

The problem solver.

The dead man.

"Figure out your tools," Norman said. "Tools are good."

At the first glance, the tool situation was sparse. He had nothing in his pockets, not even a ring of car keys, and the explosion hadn't sent anything useful his way (such as a blowtorch, or a hydraulic car jack). The only thing within reaching distance was the block of metal pinning him to the tree, and parts of that had been shorn to a razor's edge by the blast. If he leaned forward far enough, he could slice his throat open, but that was more like a "permanent solution to a temporary problem." Also, he had the roots of this tree. He could gnaw on them when he began to get hungry. He could eat tree roots and hope the fiber would give him strength until one day, when he'd eaten the entire hydration structure, he'd be strong enough to lift the wreckage off his legs and toss it away as if it were made out of feathers.

"Ain't happening," Norman said. He fingered a sharp flap of metal, a broken piece of the truck's body. Buddha had sat at the foot of a tree until he achieved enlightenment, hadn't he? A bodhi tree, or was it pine? Maybe involuntary enlightenment was Norman's destiny. Maybe he would sit here until he figured out the Despair, in fact all the world's problems. Hell, it'd be easy.

"Ha ha."

Norman bent the flap of metal in one direction, then another. He kept bending until he snapped the piece off.

Shaped like an arrowhead, the metal shard was sharp on all sides and he could only hold it by pinching it between his fingers. He could use it to fight off wild dogs. Clean his fingernails. Or cut and peel the roots around him, make his final meals easier to choke down. "Good stuff," Norman said, no longer noticing if the words were said aloud or in his head. He'd lost some blood. Had a bad shock. And now he was harvesting roots for food after his last remaining friends had been taken from him, and this tree could die along with him, goddamn it. It could die.

Norman whistled as he slashed every exposed root within reach. By the time he'd finished the sky was dark and bats whizzed over his head, heading out for the night's hunt. He piled the sap-bleeding roots on top of the wreckage and thought about peeling them, too, even though it was too dark to really see the roots anymore or the shard of metal. He counted the roots by touch. Forty-two. A solid number of roots. A heap of roots. A—

"Actually, that might work."

Norman brushed the roots off the wreckage and piled them around his waist. He stuffed as many as would fit into the gap his legs created between the wreckage and the ground below. He took a deep breath and lifted the wreckage the small amount he could manage, then used his right hand to stuff a few more roots on top of the original pile. His left hand gave out under the weight almost immediately, and the wreckage dropped back onto his lap, sending another dizzying jolt of pain up his spine. Yet, didn't there seem to be a little more space now? Wasn't the wreckage maybe a few centimeters higher than before as it sat on the piled roots?

He thought it was.

It took most of the night. Clammy fog settled over the ground, hanging low against the surrounding trees. Norman grew weak with the cold and it took longer to gather his strength between bursts of activity. But his efforts did pay off, eventually. The piled roots held up and created enough space for Norman to yank his legs out from beneath the wreckage. Once free, he rolled onto his stomach and crawled away from the place he was supposed to die. He felt his legs for breaks and found none. He kicked his legs out until blood began to circulate through them. He attempted a push-up, failed, and ended up rolling onto his back. The fog had thinned out, revealing a murky array of stars in the night sky.

"Well, got out of that, didn't I?"

The stars didn't respond. He knew they didn't care, that this entire forest didn't care whether he lived or died or went whooping through the hills buck naked with a fiery torch. Nature cared about you the way a driver cared about a bug slamming into his truck's chrome grille. That was about it.

Norman groaned and got off the ground. He stood, wobbled, then his needling legs gave out beneath him. He fell against the tree and wrapped his arms around it to keep from falling. The tree's bark smelled like moss and dirt. His nose itched as a black ant crawled across him on the way to something more important. His legs burned like hell, but he kept hugging the tree until the burn lessened. He shook his legs out, let go of the tree, and took a few small, cautious steps. This time his legs held.

"Now we're talking."

He staggered down the hillside and out of the ditch, dodging chunks of debris by the soapy light of predawn. The truck's engine lay on the edge of the road, brown water still leaking from its block. A wide crater punctured the road beyond the wreckage. He wavered on the crater's edge, leaning back on his heels and waving his arms to steady himself. The crater appeared to be about ten feet in diameter. The missile, or whatever it had been, must have clipped the truck's tail end. He called out for Zero although he could already tell the scene was deserted. He searched the ground for a telltale scrap of clothing or hair, but couldn't find anything. Hopefully she'd died upon impact, her body vaporized in the explosion. Better that than being taken prisoner by the Collectors, alive or dead.

Norman skirted the crater and continued down the road. The sun rose above the mountains. It grew warmer. He ignored the soreness in his body and drank from the first stream he came across. He walked uphill all day, listening to the birds warble for each other and counting the old mile markers he passed. At dusk he came to a small, boarded-up gas station on the side of the road. He pulled the boards away and climbed in through a window. It smelled like animal urine and scat, but what he cared about was the mostly empty shelves on the gas station's walls. All the food, canned and otherwise, had already been taken. He searched the station's storage room and found a dusty can sitting on what must have been the manager's desk. Right next to the can was a cheap can opener, as if someone else had been about to eat and then stopped. Norman picked up the can and rubbed off the dust. A fluffy white dog smiled back at him, tongue lolling. Norman set the can down and opened it. The pungent smell of rancid gravy and low-grade meat filled the storeroom. Norman dug his fingers into the can without hesitation.

Enough derelict gas stations and diners dotted the interstate to provide food and shelter for Norman as he crossed out of Oregon and entered Washington. He scavenged a down jacket, some silverware, towels, a lighter, compass, hunting knife, and a leather satchel to carry it all. He came across dozens of vehicles that would not start, but he didn't mind. The Collectors' attack had soured him on the whole motorized-transportation thing for a while.

After a few days Norman felt as if he'd been walking forever, each foot following the other through all types of wind, rain, and heat. He walked through blisters until he couldn't feel them anymore and his feet were callused and scabbed, and moving was all he did, the pavement gliding beneath him almost of its own accord. His world grew small, became simply trees and patches of highway without trees, and as long as he kept moving, he found it easy to avoid thinking about anything. He did not need to think about the litany of dead, the missing girl from Kansas he'd been responsible for guarding. He only needed to walk, and as long as he kept moving, that was enough.

During his sixth day on foot Norman ducked beneath a picnic shelter to avoid a sudden downpour. The shelter belonged to another dilapidated interstate rest stop. It was easy to imagine parked cars and RVs and minivans in the parking lot, families jumping out of vehicles as they stretched their legs and made beelines for the restrooms. All those families were gone now. Tugged under by the Despair, their members disappearing from the world one by one.

The rain didn't stop until dark. By then Norman was asleep, stretched out on a damp picnic table and covered by everything he owned.

Norman bathed every few days. He preferred ponds or lakes. He would swim as deep as possible and open his eyes, hoping to see a coral blue Atlantis among the dim murk of algae and water-lily stems.

Each time, he found nothing.

On the seventeenth day of his forced hike Norman entered a particularly dense patch of Washington forest. Several old blue spruce trees had fallen, covering the highway. He climbed across their trunks. The birds, which had been warbling all morning, suddenly fell silent as he landed back on the road. The forest to his right began shaking, branches snapping as something big pushed its way forward. Before Norman could consider the situation properly, an adult grizzly bear emerged from the trees, bounding up the highway's ditch and onto the road. It had shaggy fur, a thick hump behind its head, and a body substantial with summer fat and muscle. The bear peered at Norman.

Norman stood his ground as the bear sniffed the air cautiously. Even its round nose was huge. "Hello," Norman said. "How are ya?" The bear growled, but made no move to spring forward. Instead it reared back and sat down, as if to get a better look at Norman. Even seated, it matched his height.

"Ever seen a human before?"

The bear made a snuffing noise. Norman smiled. He wished Pops were here to see this. A grizzly the size of a mountain, sitting right in the middle of the interstate. It showed no fear of man, either. It had probably never heard gunfire or edged its way around a bear trap.

"Sir, I'm glad we've met here on this road," Norman said, folding his hands and lowering them to his waist. "You see, my people can't handle living anymore. The struggle is too much for them. They want to sleep forever, or go to heaven, or return to the earth reincarnated as plump, leaf-eating caterpillars. Whatever. The thing is, they want things they believe this world can't offer them, and since they are so busy dying out, they can no longer rule this world. Therefore the task falls to you, Noble One."

Norman unclasped his hands and knelt until his forehead touched the road. "You now possess the Invisible Crown. You are the King of the United States, the King of North America, and, above all, King of Earth. Congratulations, Your Majesty, and may your reign last a trillion years."

The bear yawned, exhaling hot, meaty air. Norman kept his forehead pressed to the road and his neck extended. The bear growled. Would it bite him in the neck, or would it have at him with its paws? He thought about Jordan as the bear rocked in place and regained its legs. It swayed closer, its front paws scraping inches away. Looking sidelong, Norman could make out the tip of each sharp, black claw.

The bear sniffed the top of Norman's head. The new ruler of earth smelled like a mixture of dirt, pine needles, and wet dog. Norman shivered as the bear growled again. He saw that his own fingernails were long, ridiculously long, and that a ladybug had crawled out of a crack in the road and was headed for his right pinkie.

The bear snuffed and turned back to the woods. Norman could hear the clacking of the bear's long nails on the road as it walked, a sound that reminded him of the black Lab his family had once owned.

It had been a good dog.

A good life.

More walking. More hot weather, more mosquitoes, and more food raids on dusty convenience stores. Each day like the one before it and the one ahead, the only difference between them the gradually changing scenery. Mt. Rainier appeared in the distance, a formidable, snowcapped mountain far to the west, and the road began to flatten out. One warm, humid day Norman came to a long stretch of road without trees. The sky was clear, and it was easy to imagine a helicopter swooping down, guns firing. Norman pulled up and squinted at the horizon.

"Good place for an ambush."

He wiped his forehead with the back of his hand. The ditch crickets were out in force today, droning on and on and on. The sound had grown so familiar to Norman that he didn't notice it anymore. Like static noise, keeping time to your heartbeat.

"Any Collectors around?" Norman shouted, cupping his hands around his mouth. "Planning another ambush, maybe?"

He waited, but no helicopters. The ditch weeds and wildflowers swayed in the wind but no helicopters, no death from above. Norman continued down the highway. It was so bright today even his scavenged sunglasses couldn't keep the glare out. He turned to the sun as he walked, closing his eyes to absorb the light through his eyelids. He whistled an old tune, some song his father had loved, and when he opened his eyes again, a man was crossing the road ahead of him, traveling from east to west. Around forty years old, the man was dressed in a tattered gray business suit and carried a brown leather suitcase.

"Hello," Norman called out. The businessman kept his

eyes straight ahead, his face visible only in profile. After he crossed the road, the businessman stepped down into the tall weeds and disappeared.

"Hey! Wait a second!"

Two more people, women this time, stepped out of the field to his right. Both of them blond and sharp-jawed, they could have been sisters. They wore yellow sundresses and straw hats. They didn't answer Norman's shouts as they crossed the road, either, didn't glance his way.

"Ah," Norman said, wiping his hands on his pants. "So this is what it's like to go crazy. Always wondered."

Four children, two boys and two girls, stepped out of the weeds. This time Norman ran right up to them and shouted into their small ears. They did not start at his approach or do anything other than stare straight ahead as they walked, eyes focused on something to the west.

"Nice day, isn't it?"

Norman wanted to yank one of the boys aside by the arm and demand a few answers, but he didn't. The children appeared untouchable. Like ghosts. "Okay then," Norman said, stepping back. The ghost children crossed the road and stepped down into the weeds, disappearing like the others. Norman pinched his cheek as more folks appeared. Dozens of people. Men, women, children. Dressed in all types of clothes. Bonnets. Suits. Khaki shorts and yellow raincoats. Like an eerie, silent fashion show they crossed the road, passing around Norman before disappearing into the opposite field. Norman stopped calling out to them, knowing he'd get no response beyond the

blood pounding in his ears. They didn't want to talk to him. Maybe they couldn't. They had their own journey to make. A different sort of conversation.

Norman stood in the road for hours as hundreds more passed him by. He did not want to leave these people behind, unnoticed by a living soul as they made their way west. Eventually the last person, a bent old man leaning on a cane, crossed the road, and the parade was over. "The end," Norman said, and started walking again. He made it about a mile before he collapsed face-first onto the simmering road.

His head pounded.

He needed water.

Shade.

Instead, Norman lay there thinking about lemmings. The idea that lemmings were suicidal was a popular misconception. Lemmings did not purposefully kill themselves. During times of severe overpopulation they simply picked a random direction and headed for a new environment. They did not knowingly hurl themselves off cliffs or run into the sea. If a lemming was killed during the migration, it was because it found itself in unfamiliar territory and was usually pushed to its death by members of its own species. What if the Despair worked like that, too? What if humanity as a whole was meant to migrate somewhere else, and its members had simply fallen off a path they couldn't understand in the first place?

Norman pulled his coat over his head. He dug out a bottle of water from his satchel. He poured some water over his head and drank the rest. The migrant ghost people had been

hallucinations brought on by dehydration. Sunstroke. He'd be okay. Needed some rest, was all. He laid his head on the leather satchel and curled up on his side. Despite the hot Duracrete road and the exposed nature of his position, Norman drifted off easily. He dreamed he was sleeping with his wife and her hair smelled like oil and warm leather, and when he kissed her neck, it was hard and metallic, like a brass buckle, and then suddenly he was standing in the middle of a vast crowd, everyone watching him, waiting to see what he would do, so he reached up and pulled a white rabbit out of his hat.

After his sun sickness Norman mostly traveled at night, preferring to sleep while the summer sun bore down on Washington. The muscles in Norman's legs had hardened, his stomach had shrunk, and his back was feeling stronger than it had since college. Norman met only a handful of other living people along the interstate, and when they saw him, they ran into the overgrown forests and could not be coaxed out. After receiving no answer for such a long time, Norman stopped calling after the vaguely human shapes that occasionally peered at him from the woods, inspecting him as he passed.

Beyond midsummer Norman came across a well-maintained brick house within sight of the interstate. The house sat at the end of a gravel road and was illuminated by a nearly full moon. Norman scanned the house's windows for light and saw none. When he neared the house, Norman

shouted hello and made as much noise as possible. The lawn was dotted with porcelain birdbaths, granite angels, and un-. settling, pointy-headed gnomes. Norman walked up the front steps and knocked on the front door. The knocking was obnoxiously loud in the middle of such a quiet night, but nothing stirred inside the house. He tried the doorknob. It turned without hesitation and the door swung inward. Norman sniffed the air for the smell of a decomposing body, but he could only smell dust and a hint of something vanilla, maybe a candle.

He found no dead bodies anywhere in the house. The living room was tidy. The dining room was tidy. The kitchen was tidy. Norman riffled through the kitchen cabinets until he found a bottle of whiskey. He poured himself a drink and sat down at the kitchen table. It was nice being in a house again, to have a roof over his head and a comfortable chair to sit in. He finished his drink, his stomach warm, and made his way up to the second floor of the house. He found a bedroom with the bed already made, and the air smelled like dried flowers and pinecones, some type of homemade potpourri. He slid into bed like a good little Goldilocks. It was almost dawn, the end of the day in his new, nocturnal schedule. His bones and muscles felt heavy, tired of propelling him day after day down the hard surface of America's decaying road system. He yawned and rolled onto his side.

What kind of people had lived in this room? Had they lived here before the Despair or had they squatted here, escaping another place where the past was too heavy for them to bear? Had they somehow eked out moments of happiness during the last five years? Experienced little spots of humor and joy that allowed them to forget the worst, if only for a minute? Would they know him if they met him on the road, would they smile and say, "Hey, you look familiar. Didn't you once stay in our home?"

The next evening Norman started down the road again, and soon another week was behind him. He stopped counting mile markers. Doing the math. He didn't want to know how many miles he had gone. They didn't matter, any more than time mattered. He thought about Jordan, Pops, Zero, and he spent hours trying to remember them down to exact details, down to the oil beneath Pops' fingernails and the way Zero chewed on a strand of her hair when she was thinking about something. He wondered for the thousandth time if the girl was still alive, and, if so, what did the Collectors have in mind for her? Another victim of sacrifice, like Cardenio? A possible Collector protégé? No. She was dead. The girl had to be dead.

Norman stopped sleeping at regular intervals. Dark or light no longer mattered to him, and the road became one long blur as one day lost any sense of division from the next. He stopped only when he was exhausted and slept wherever he was standing at that moment. He ate scavenged food and drank water only to keep his body moving, ignoring the taste of whatever he consumed. He was bitten by endless swarms of mosquitoes, but his skin was so rough now, so covered in old bites and other scabs, that he didn't notice.

Norman reached the abandoned outskirts of Seattle by the beginning of autumn. He hadn't eaten anything for three days. Despite a misting rain, smoke rose from the city center in fat, spiraling coils. Norman recalled the drifter he'd met back in Florida. The way he'd spoken of Dr. Briggs and the scientist's search for a cure. The drifter's gleaming eyes.

PART FOUR

Coastland

18

The city had burned.

Fire had come through Seattle like hell's own hurricane and gutted it, leaving a blackened, still-cooling inferno of exposed girders, soot-covered sidewalks, and roofless, partially collapsed buildings. Norman walked down the city's smoldering boulevards and tried not to laugh. He was worried if he started laughing, he would never be able to stop and he would spend the rest of his life cackling in the smoky ruins of downtown Seattle, starving and exposed to the elements.

He circled a burning car, giving it a wide berth in case it exploded. Burning chemical smells hung over the city in pockets, each one different and slightly more lung scorching than the last. Norman tied a handkerchief over his face as rain continued to fall in a light mist. The next street looked even worse, piled thick with more flaming cars and trucks, and the smell of burning tires and battery acid made his eyes water. He wondered how close he had come to witnessing

Seattle's last great fire, the fiery deluge that would finally drop the coastal city to its knees. Had it been two days, maybe three?

Norman came to an overpass covered in faded graffiti as the clouded sky began to darken. He touched the painted words with his hand.

She is gone, and soon I will be, too. Do
not pray for us, and do not weep.
Simply cry a little, for our souls to keep.

This is not suicide
   This is not suicide
      This is setting yourself

              Free

We understand now, Kurt.
We understand.

   I hear the humming of
angels and I will be with them
     Soon
   I will sing I will
    not be dead
    I will be
   more alive
than ever before.

Norman slumped against the overpass and fell asleep, glad at least to be out of the rain.

It had rained hard during the night and many of the remaining fires had been extinguished. Norman emerged from beneath the overpass, washed his face in a puddle of rainwater, and headed toward the one definable Seattle landmark he'd always wanted to visit: the Space Needle.

The Needle sat almost a mile beyond Seattle's downtown district, to the northwest. Its tall, thin base and haloed head appeared untouched by the fires, an aging monument designed to withstand hurricane-force winds and major earthquakes. The closer Norman got to the Space Needle the taller it appeared, and by the time he reached the grassy lawn surrounding its base he felt slightly dizzy looking up at it. Several round hills surrounded the Needle's base, some as high as forty feet. Norman climbed one and lay down, reclining on his elbows as he listened to the Needle creak with the wind. He considered the hills around him, obviously man-made, and realized he was lying on one of several burial mounds. Mounds that went back, he supposed, to the beginning of the Despair.

He slid down the hill and headed toward the Space Needle's entrance. The doors had been torn off and the entryway was covered with graffiti, more faded messages. The lights were off and nothing happened when he pushed any of the elevator buttons. He found a door that led to a flight of stairs. The

stairway was dark, lacking even emergency lighting. Norman
dug around in his satchel and retrieved a flashlight. It gave off
a dim yellow light, but it was enough to see by as he made his
way up the stairs, counting each flight along the way.

After about sixty floors Norman reached the enclosed interior of the Needle's observation deck. He sat down on a bench,
breathing hard. He took in the numerous maps that had once
conveyed points of interest to tourists, their unlit, plastic sur-
faces coated with dust. Here, more than anywhere else he'd
visited on his journey, the silence created by the Despair
seemed loudest. Just a few years ago, thousands of visitors
from all over the world had passed through here every day,
warming the observation deck with their heat and shutterbug
noise, and now their absence lingered in the air like the faded
energy resonance normally found in ancient cathedrals.

When his breathing returned to normal, Norman stood
up from the bench and opened one of several doors ringing
the Needle's circular interior. He stepped out onto the observation deck. Most of the deck's wire safety fencing had been
torn away, leaving the view open and unhindered. To the
south of the Needle sat Seattle's charred and desolate downtown district, a forest of smoking skyscrapers nestled against
the shore of Elliott Bay. The bay itself was brilliant with re-
flected sunlight, and a few rusted freight ships sat rocking on
its surface, as if waiting to continue some unfinished journey. Beyond the city, the distant blue smudge of Mt. Rainier.

Norman yawned. His empty stomach was so acidic he
hardly felt like eating at all. The wind came up and the Space

Needle creaked, swaying and catching Norman off guard. He pitched forward against the concrete rail, leaning over just far enough to see why the wire-mesh safety netting had been a good idea. He also saw a word of graffiti that he wouldn't have noticed otherwise. It simply said

WATERFRONT

and unlike the other graffiti Norman had seen throughout the city, the paint on this message was fresh, a bright forest green that stood out against the concrete barrier's outer side. And if the paint was fresh, the message was fresh.

"Hell," Norman said, rubbing his palms on his jeans. "Guess that means more walking." He turned away from the view and headed for the Needle's dank stairway. At least it was easier going down than up.

More simmering debris, blasted-out cars, and buckled chunks of sidewalk. Downtown Seattle was an even more hellish maze than the city's outer regions, and Norman passed uninjured through the rubble only because his hunger and overall exhaustion made him move so slowly, like an old man picking his way through the world's largest junkyard. The afternoon sky clouded, rained, and cleared again while he walked, his eyes on his feet as he gradually approached Elliott Bay. He came across the same WATERFRONT message two more times, also freshly spray-painted in forest green, on the bottom of an overturned school bus and on the front of a burned-out Jewish temple.

The sun began to set as Norman wandered through what remained of Seattle's shipyards. He stopped to lean against an electrical pole and consider his bleak sleeping options for the evening. A coal blue pigeon landed near his feet. He kicked at it, but the pigeon just fluttered into the air and settled again a couple feet away. Norman scowled. The pigeon was so fat. What business did it have looking so vibrant and alive? Now it was preening its feathers. Really nibbling at them.

"Hey," Norman said. "You there."

Norman knelt and sifted through the char around his feet. He found a stone and it warmed the palm of his hand. Fat bird like that would taste better than air for supper. Norman chucked the stone as hard as he could. It missed the pigeon by several feet and struck an overturned vending machine, rattling off the machine's shrunken plastic skin. The bird cooed and continued its grooming. He stomped at it, waving his hands. The pigeon waited until Norman's shadow fell over it before fluttering back a few feet and cooing some more. Norman rushed it again, with the same result. He searched the ground for another stone as the pigeon pecked at the soil around it, oblivious to the human's efforts. Where were all the good throwing stones when you needed them? All this damn rubble, you'd think there'd be something good.

The pigeon pulled a chubby, pink worm out of the soil and waved it proudly in the air. Norman forgot his search for a stone and charged the bird, shouting obscenities as he ran. The pigeon flapped its wings and skittered away, bouncing between the air and the ground as it headed for the nearest building, a warehouse that was missing its fourth wall, as well as its roof. Norman chased the bird into the warehouse, his hands curled into claws. The waning sunlight filtered into the open building from above, illuminating an enormous mound of sand piled in the building's center, where hundreds of other pigeons congregated, pecking at the sand. Some were brilliantly colored, teal-headed and white-breasted, but most of the pigeons were dun brown, or a dull, listless gray. The pigeon he'd been chasing, the coal blue one with the juicy worm, joined its brethren on the sand pile and was instantly hidden by the throng. Norman kept running anyway, determined to dive into the pile, snap a few necks, and bring home some dinner. He ran hard, but as he was about to pounce, he slipped in a puddle of bird shit and lost his balance. He turned on his heels and fell backward into the sand pile.

A few pigeons hopped away, but the rest kept on scratching with their ugly toes, digging into the sand. Norman made a croaking sound that slowly grew into a laugh. He gazed up at the sky where a roof should have been and laughed at the gray clouds above, promising more rain. He made a sand angel, then realized it wasn't sand.

It was birdseed.

Why would there be a massive pile of birdseed here, in this deserted warehouse? It seemed fresh, too. Something like this would attract birds, hundreds of birds, and hundreds of birds might attract a fair amount of attention. Norman leaned up on his elbows and scanned the warehouse. Empty, except for a few piles of metal twisted beyond recognition. He glanced higher and his eyes fell on a banner hanging over the warehouse entrance, its lettering also in forest green.

```
Thank You for Coming
We'll Be with You Soon
```

Beneath the banner was a small, red-eyed surveillance camera. Norman waved to the camera and fell back against the birdseed. Something tight in his back, a tourniquet wound deep, loosened as he continued laughing.

"That's a long trip," she said. "Why Seattle?"

"I came to see the wizard."

"Wizard?"

"Dr. Briggs. I came to see Dr. Briggs."

The pair exchanged a look. Norman's stomach gurgled, making a sound like oxygen bubbles rising in a watercooler.

"Happily, Dr. Briggs survived the fires," the man said. "If you'd like to come with us, we could see about a meeting."

"Sure. I'd appreciate that."

They led Norman across the warehouse floor and into a freight elevator. The woman punched a code into a numeric keypad and the elevator began a slow, rickety descent. When they reached the bottom, they got off. Their footfalls echoed on the linoleum as they passed through corridors painted in bright yellows, greens, and blues. Children had taped up paper cutouts to the walls, creating a colorful mosaic of smiling bunnies, puppies, dinosaurs, flowers, clouds, and teddy bears. They turned down a hallway that smelled like coffee and baking bread. The occasional sign said things like BE VIGILANT and PLEASE DON'T DO IT: DIAL #726 FOR HELP. Classical music played softly, drifting down from speakers Norman could not see.

"Quite the setup," Norman said, glancing down yet another long corridor. "What was this place originally?"

"Dr. Briggs worked as a scientist in this underground complex before the Despair," the man said. "This was a secret government laboratory, housing three hundred researchers and their assistants. When the Despair began, Dr. Briggs locked himself in his lab with a supply of food and simply

19

Norman didn't have to wait long. Two people, a man and a woman, emerged from a shadowy corner of the warehouse a few minutes after he waved at the camera. Neither appeared armed. The man had silvery hair, broad shoulders, and a soft, rounded face. The woman was tall and dark-skinned, with a burn scar running from her cheek to her throat. Norman stood and brushed the birdseed from his clothes.

"Evening," the man said.

Norman nodded back. "Evening."

The woman examined Norman, taking in his dirty face and soot-covered clothes. "You survived the fires, sir?"

"Not exactly. Just got into town yesterday. Came up from Florida."

"Florida," the man said. "May we ask your name?"

"Norman."

The man glanced at his partner. Her eyes remained focused on Norman.

concentrated on his work. After a year passed, Dr. Briggs went back aboveground, found other survivors, and organized them. He not only formed a surface headquarters up above, but restocked this underground facility as well, in case of emergency."

Norman stopped. "He's been working on a cure, right? An antidote to the Despair?"

"Pure myth," the man said. "Dr. Briggs's work has nothing to do with the Despair itself."

"But the drifters—"

"They are misguided. Myths spread, especially myths people want to hear."

"So there's no Cure?"

"No."

Norman's hands balled into fists. He drew his arm back to throw a punch at the wall, at the goddamn injustice of it all, but the woman caught his arm before the punch was thrown. She twisted it behind his back and dropped him to his knees. The pain forced tears to his eyes. "Please, Norman," she whispered in his ear. "We cannot permit violence in this facility. Emotional equilibrium must be maintained."

"Won't do it again," Norman gasped.

She let go of his arm. The man helped Norman to his feet and they continued walking in a world without a Cure. Norman's arm burned in its socket, but it wasn't broken. At least the pain distracted him from his stomach, which felt as if it were starting to digest itself. His escorts stopped at an open doorway and turned to him. "Your room," the woman said.

"Food will arrive shortly. We will inform Dr. Briggs of your arrival, and he may be able to meet with you in the morning."

"Thanks," Norman said. "This was fun."

His escorts nodded and turned back down the corridor. Norman shut the door to his bedroom. A dusty king-size bed sat in the middle of the room, a mustard yellow armchair in the far corner, next to a standing lamp. Mismatched, over-varnished end tables. A cheap wooden writing desk. Norman dropped backward onto the enormous bed and kicked off his boots. His swollen feet were hardly recognizable as feet anymore. How would he get them back in his shoes?

Someone knocked on his door.

"It's unlocked."

A woman entered carrying a tray of food. She was petite with short red hair, green eyes, and white, jagged scars on her wrists. Norman guessed she was in her late twenties, early thirties.

"Norman, right?"

"That's me."

"I'm Maria. Welcome to our little home away from home. It's not much, but at least it's heavily fortified."

Norman sat up on the edge of the bed. Maria handed him the tray and sat down beside him. She smelled like soap. Norman wondered how bad he smelled. Smoke, ash, and worse clung to his clothes and skin. Seattle smoldered above them, and he was about to eat a bowl of corn chowder.

"Go ahead," Maria said, patting his knee. "Don't mind me. I ate earlier."

Norman tried to eat slowly, so he wouldn't vomit the soup back up. He was so malnourished he could feel the hollowness in his bones, in the desiccated length of his tongue. One spoonful and he nearly gagged it all up again.

"Poor guy," Maria said. "You're all skin and bones. Like a prisoner of war, almost."

"Good food. Can't remember a better meal, really."

"Thank you. I made the chowder myself. I can't tell you how good it is to see a fresh face around here. A girl gets sick of looking at the same people all the time."

Norman worked on the bread and soup until he finished both. His stomach hurt, but it was a good hurt. He gave the tray back to Maria.

"So. What happened?"

Maria ran a hand through her hair. "You mean, up above? They came, Seattle burned, and twenty thousand people died."

Norman hunched over, elbows on knees. "They?"

"The Collectors. Placed firebombs throughout the city, very strategic like, and set them all off at once. Dr. Briggs says a squadron of U.S. fighter jets couldn't have done a more thorough job."

Norman's stomach lurched up. He fought it back down again. Sweat trickled down his face despite the cold. "But the Collectors don't attack people. They just take away the dead."

Maria's weight shifted on the bed. She put a light hand on his back. "We thought so, too. Guess that's changed. Maybe they got tired of waiting around for the rest of us to pass and decided to finish the job themselves. Personally, I think Seattle was starting to do so well it made them nervous."

Another stab of pain. Norman clutched his stomach and held it. The red-haired woman quietly waited with him as he focused on breathing. The pain sharpened, then withdrew. Norman let go of his stomach and straightened up.

"Thanks for the soup, Maria, but I'm pretty tired."

Maria sprang up from the bed. "Of course you are. Here, let me fold the blankets back for you. Do you have enough pillows? I could get you more. And what about blankets?"

Norman waved her off. "I slept beneath an overpass last night. This bed will feel like heaven."

"Okay, then, let me help you out of those disgusting clothes." Maria lifted Norman's shirt over his head before he could argue. "Lift those arms—good, good—and what about those greasy blue jeans?"

"Um," Norman said, still struggling out of his shirt as Maria unbuttoned his pants and slid them off.

"No need to be shy here, Norman. It's nothing I haven't seen before."

"Okay . . ."

Norman flinched as the woman removed his underwear. He slid into bed, covering his nakedness with blankets. Maria clapped her hands.

"Anything else you need? A glass of water, maybe?"

"Uh, no, thanks. I'm fine. Really."

Maria bundled his dirty clothes under one arm and carried the plastic food tray in the other. "Shout if you need anything during the night."

"I will."

Maria opened the door and stepped into the hallway. She reached back in and flicked off the lights.

"Good night, Norman. I'm glad you're here."

"Thanks."

The red-haired woman shut the door and the room darkened. Norman dropped his head back against a pillow. A real, honest-to-God feather pillow. His body felt like stone. Immovable. He was ready to sleep for the next thousand years.

No Cure.

20

Norman woke in a pitch-black vault. Twisted blankets and lumpy, sweat-drenched pillows were the entire world, even as he came to the edge of his bed and looked beyond it. He grunted and got to his feet, kneading the thick carpet with his toes. He felt his way through the dark and found a small bathroom attached to his room. He turned the light on. The bathroom had a shower. An honest-to-God shower. How long had it been? How many months? Norman turned the water on, expecting the worst, but the showerhead surged to life with warm water. He stepped into the stall and shut the door behind him. Steam filled the stall and he dunked his head under the water.

"Yeah," Norman said. "This is good."

Norman leaned into the showerhead's hot spray as his muscles relaxed. His thoughts drifted from Florida to Kansas to the twenty thousand people who had, until recently, lived aboveground in Seattle.

At first, twenty thousand people seemed faceless and un-knowable, like all the other numbers that had once been reported on the TV news and streamed across the Web, numbers that had grown so fast you could not grasp them all. Only with effort could Norman imagine an individual citizen of Seattle, then another. The trick was details. If you gave each number details, little quirks and personality traits, then you slowly came to a recognizable, breathing person. Norman imagined one person who was overweight, reclusive, and short-tempered. Then he imagined a second person who was tall, big-boned, and had an acidic sense of humor. A little girl, sallow and weak-eyed, born after humanity had already given up on the future. Norman imagined a dozen people more, of all shapes, colors, and sizes. All of them had their own methods of dealing with the Despair, their own defense mechanisms that had allowed them to live long enough to be murdered.

Water poured down Norman's face.

His blood warmed.

After showering, Norman dressed in a clean T-shirt and new blue jeans someone (Maria?) had left on his writing desk. He left his room and called out for help. No one responded, so he started down the dim hallway on his own, deciding to find Dr. Briggs himself. As he passed the domestic units, his footsteps bounced off the tiled floor and concrete ceiling with an uncanny, cavernlike echo. After five years of lawlessness, it was oddly reassuring to be around so much government money, evidence that millions of taxpayers had once all contributed to secret projects of which they had no true conception.

He came to a T in the corridor. He picked the hallway that was more brightly lit and followed it until he came to a door with Dr. Briggs's nameplate. The nameplate was classic wood-panel brown, with the doctor's name in white lettering. Norman wondered if the government had given Briggs the nameplate on his first day of work, or if he'd earned it after years of research and departmental politics. The door swung open as Norman knocked. He shouted hello, received no answer, and stepped inside.

The lab wasn't as big or as mad-scientist-like as Norman expected. The ceiling was only about twelve feet high, the walls painted beige, and most of the equipment sat on orderly rows of wire shelving. The floor was carpeted, a plush blue fiber that sprang up underfoot like grass. On the far end of the room several tables were littered with a variety of tools and equipment, almost all of which Norman had never before seen. Norman walked farther into the lab and found the scientist at the other end of the room, reclining in a leather chair and wrapped in an afghan. Dr. Briggs's eyes were closed. A small Asian man, he appeared roughly fifty years old. He had closely cropped white hair and smooth, finely boned hands. A wooden cane the color of black cherries rested across his lap. The cane was lacquered and had a carved duck's head for a handle. So here was the man, the myth, the legend. Taking a snooze.

Norman gently shook the scientist's shoulder. "Dr. Briggs?"

"Hmmm?"

"My name is Norman, sir. I arrived last night from Florida."

"Florida."

"Yes, sir. I'd like to talk with you."

The scientist's eyes opened and scanned the room, taking in the entire lab before they settled on Norman. "I apologize, Norman. You have caught me napping. I've been rather exhausted this last week."

"I can understand that."

The scientist sat forward but made no move to rise. "Yes, Norman, I am sure you can relate quite well. Please, sit down."

Norman sat in the overstuffed armchair beside the scientist's recliner. Dr. Briggs took off his glasses and polished them with his shirt. "You've come a long way to see me. After all the rumors, you must feel rather disappointed with the whole operation."

"You could say that."

"Actually, we've heard reports about you, too, Norman. About your standoff with the Collectors."

"Reports?"

Dr. Briggs finished polishing his glasses and put them back on. "A motorcycle messenger arrived several weeks ago from Kansas City. Like you, he'd come to confirm rumors of a cure. He left us only a few days before the firebombings to return home."

"One of the Mayor's men."

"Yes. May I ask if his story was accurate? Did you recently shoot a Collector?"

Norman rubbed his hands together. He recalled the heavy feel of the shotgun. The pressure of his index finger against the trigger, the thudding recoil into his shoulder.

"I did," Norman said. "They would have taken my wife's body."

Norman expected follow-up questions to this answer, but Dr. Briggs didn't say anything, simply nodded his head and turned his cane between his hands, grinding its tip into the carpeted floor. One of the machines in the lab beeped twice before falling silent again as the ventilation system kicked on overhead.

"Have you noticed the signs posted in the corridors, Norman?"

"The ones that read BE VIGILANT and DON'T DO IT?"

"Yes. The phone number on each sign connects whoever calls it to our own internal suicide hotline. Within five minutes, anyone who dials that number is rushed to our care center for treatment. Sometimes this treatment merely involves cookies, powdered milk, and an attentive listener. Sometimes it involves more than that."

Norman wondered if another afghan was lying around, something to offset the chilly, filtered air blowing down from the ceiling. He couldn't imagine living underground like this. No windows, and all the air recycled.

"We also have a buddy system. Each person living in the

complex has two buddies who are on call to that person twenty-four hours a day. Whenever someone feels the least bit suicidal, they are required to seek out their buddies and share their feelings. As you can imagine, this creates a strong bond and helps reinforce even the bleakest souls among us.

"Yet, while these measures have been reasonably successful, we still lose people. At least one person slips away a week, and since the fires that number has increased to one every eight hours. If this rate continues, by the end of this calendar year the complex will undoubtedly be empty of human life."

Dr. Briggs cleared his throat.

"Norman, do you remember seeing ships anchored in Elliott Bay?"

"Yeah. The freighters."

"One of those ships is still in operation. A Collector vessel. It pulled in a day after the fires began, and they've been hauling bodies away ever since. At least, the bodies that haven't been completely cremated."

Dr. Briggs paused to let his words sink in.

Norman hunched over in his chair and ran his hands through his hair. "On our way here, in Oregon, they killed my friend, and I think they kidnapped the girl we were traveling with. A girl named Zero."

"I'm sorry to hear that."

"Do you think there's any chance she's on that ship?"

Dr. Briggs frowned. "It's possible. Seattle seems to be their central collection point for the entire Pacific Northwest. Whether the girl remains alive or not is an entirely different matter, of course. Four days ago, the Collectors essentially declared war on the living. They do not seem to be the type to grant quarter."

"No," Norman said. "They don't."

Dr. Briggs shifted in his seat. "But it isn't all bleak, Norman. When I heard the report of someone killing a trespassing Collector, a light went off in my head. I thought to myself, 'Now here is someone who will stand up and help us fight back.' Really, I did. How many stories do you hear of someone fighting when the Collectors come to take away the bodies of their loved ones?"

Norman shrugged.

"Not many, I guess."

Dr. Briggs smiled. "You are unique, Norman. An anomaly. You are not merely enduring the Despair, not only surviving it, but actually engaged in an active resistance. I'd been working on the assumption that the Collectors emit a sort of white noise that paralyzes the human mind, the much reported 'humming,' but it seems that you may be uniquely wired to at least partially withstand the white noise and act despite it."

The ventilated air kicked off. Norman crossed his arms. "Where's this headed, Dr. Briggs?"

Dr. Briggs planted his cane and pushed himself out of his chair. Norman followed the scientist to the nearest worktable. On the table, sitting in a cardboard egg carton, were what appeared to be four small grenades.

"This is what I've been working on these past five years, Norman. Modified grenades."

"Modified?" Norman asked, bending over the carton. "Modified how?"

"They've been significantly compressed, the result being that each one now packs a punch a thousand times greater than a conventional grenade. In fact, just one of these is powerful enough to destroy this entire facility. I call them density grenades."

"Hell."

"Hell, indeed." Dr. Briggs picked up one of grenades and felt its weight in his hand. He handed it to Norman. "I may not have a medicinal cure for the Despair, Norman, but I can offer you the next best thing. They've declared war against the living, and if it's war they want, we'll bring it to their door. What you're holding is a shot at destroying the Collectors. A shot at, perhaps, ending the Despair itself."

Norman squeezed the grenade in his hand and pictured Jordan lying curled in their bed, her body pale and unmoving in the gloom of their bedroom. Her skin had already cooled. Become rubbery to the touch.

"What's your plan?"

21

Norman rested for three days, consuming vitamins and hot meals while running over the plan with Dr. Briggs. When Norman was not eating or training, he was sleeping, and by the third day he felt his strength return. Dr. Briggs suggested he remain in the complex another week, to fully rest up, but Norman dreamed only of fire now and understood time was short, shorter than anyone had guessed.

On the night before his departure they had a good-bye party for Norman in the complex cafeteria. He felt as if he were attending his own wake as two hundred people packed the room, shaking Norman's hand and thanking him. "This was my father's lucky watch," one boy said, pressing a pocket watch into Norman's hand. "Take it with you, please. For good luck." Norman palmed the pocket watch and put it in his pocket. "I want you to have this," a woman said, smiling as she put a silver cross necklace around Norman's neck. "It doesn't matter if you're a Christian or not. The angels pro-

tect everyone, honey. Everyone." A scruffy-bearded fat man gave Norman a bear hug and lifted him off the floor. Norman felt his shoulder dampen as the man cried on his shoulder. "We owe you, man. We owe you big-time."

Dr. Briggs stood at Norman's side during these greetings. He pointed out people with the tip of his cane, introducing each well-wisher in turn. Kids darted through the crowd and stopped to stare. Finally, the line tapered off.

"What do you think?" Dr. Briggs asked, leaning forward on his cane. "Aren't they a beautiful group?"

Norman nodded. "They're great."

"They've lost everything imaginable. Almost no one here has a surviving family member with them. In fact, many have lost the new friends they've established since the beginning of the Despair. They are the fragments of Seattle's once numerous population, yet they don't seem entirely broken, do they?"

Norman scanned the cafeteria again. A table of people near them was laughing as an old woman waved her arms wildly, imitating the old man beside her. The old man blushed while the rest of the table applauded.

"No," Norman admitted. "Looks like they've got some miles left in them."

After dessert Norman left the cafeteria to return to his room. Maria, the red-haired woman who'd tucked him in his first night in the complex, was waiting for him outside

his bedroom door. She wore a short navy blue dress, black open-toed sandals, and six silver bracelets on each wrist. The bracelets were supposed to distract, but they only accented the jagged scars beneath them. Maria smiled when she noticed him approaching and leaned her slender body against his door. Norman thought he might sleep with this woman tonight. He hoped his wife, or at least his memory of her, would understand.

"Hi, Norman."

"Evening, Maria. Spying on my room?"

She grinned and drummed her hands on the door. "You know. Watching out for bad guys. Make sure nobody sabotages anything during your good-bye dinner."

"Sabotages?"

"You know. Steals your boots. I mean, where would you be without your boots? You couldn't go anywhere."

Norman smiled and scratched the side of his head. "Thanks, I appreciate that."

He caught a whiff of Maria's perfume. A sweet, airy mix of citrus and lemon. The thought occurred to him that he'd most likely never again smell a woman's perfume after tonight. Jordan had worn rosewater perfume (beneath her earlobes, on each wrist, and a dab on her throat), but she was gone now, unable to wear any type of perfume at all, and she'd been the one to walk out on him.

"Would you like to come in, Maria?"

"If you don't mind. You're the one leaving tomorrow, Norman. You're calling the shots."

"I'd love some company."

Norman ran his keycard through and opened the door. They entered the room to find a bouquet of artificial roses, an opened bottle of red wine, and two wineglasses on Norman's writing desk. "Hey," Maria said. "The hero's send-off."

Norman laughed. "You did all this?"

"Nope. I didn't plan that far ahead. I'm just happy you asked me in. Must have been Dr. Briggs."

"Dr. Briggs?"

"Well, I told him I might stop by and talk to you tonight. Man, that guy is so wily. Do you mind if I use your bathroom?"

"Go ahead."

Norman poured the wine while Maria used the bathroom. He noticed a handwritten note beneath the bottle.

Ah, fill the Cup: What boots it to repeat
How Time is slipping underneath our Feet:
Unborn To-morrow and dead Yesterday,
Why fret about them if To-day be sweet!

Norman folded the note and stuck it in his pocket. Maria returned from the bathroom. They sat down on the edge of his bed.

"What is it, Norman? You look funny."

Norman handed Maria her glass of wine and held up his own. "Here's to life. Both the good and the bad."

"To life."

They clinked glasses and drank. Norman downed half his glass in one swallow and took another. His face warmed.

"I'm glad you're here, Maria."

"Me, too."

"You know, my wife passed this spring."

Maria set her drink down and leaned forward. She kissed him on the cheek, then on the mouth.

Norman smiled. "What did I do to earn that?"

"You're a good guy. That's what."

Norman kissed her back. Her lips were warm. Lush. He went to kiss her again, but Maria turned her head away.

"What's wrong?"

"Before we do anything, Norman, I need to tell you something. I used to be a Collector."

Norman slid off the bed and stood up. "What?"

Maria ran a hand through her red hair, jangling her bracelets. "Yeah, can you believe it? Me, running around in one of those dark robes? Those things were hot, heavy, and ugly. The three sins of bad fashion."

Maria laughed. Norman glanced at the door.

"Norman, don't look like that. This isn't some trap, if that's what you're thinking. Dr. Briggs knows all about me. I just thought I'd be honest with you before anything . . . you know, happened. Will you please sit back down?"

Norman checked the door again, still not convinced a swarm of dark robes weren't about to burst through the door and kick the living shit out of him.

"You were a Collector? As in past tense?"

"Yes."

"What happened? Why aren't you a Collector anymore?"

Maria took a drink of wine and patted the bed. "Please, Norman."

Norman refilled his wineglass and sat back down.

Maria took a breath. "When the Despair started, I was working as a cashier in a grocery store in Astoria. This was maybe within the first month after the Tokyo suicides. I didn't have the greatest job, and I hadn't had the greatest life, either. So, like a lot of people, I decided to kill myself."

Maria set her drink down. She slid her bracelets off her wrists, one by one, and let them fall onto the carpet in a tinkling pile. She fingered the red, crisscrossing scar tissue on her left wrist.

"I used a straight razor I'd inherited from my grandfather. It had a pearl handle, and I resharpened its blade for the occasion. I filled the bathtub with warm water, cried a little, and then I hacked away at my wrists, trying to hit all the big chords. It didn't really hurt that much, but it looked scary, my blood filling up our white tub like that. I fainted pretty quick.

"When I woke up, my wrists were wrapped in gauze. I was in bed. My bed. My husband was sitting by a window. I could tell he hadn't been sleeping, and I was about to say something, something like 'I'm sorry, sweetie,' when I noticed the humming in my head."

Norman blinked as Maria fingered the scars on her wrists. "Humming? You heard something hum?"

Maria nodded. "It was terrible, but sort of beautiful, too. Almost like a dream, or a vision, and it didn't go away. It hummed on and on. Like an angels' choir. And even when my wrists healed, the humming didn't go away. I knew I was being called. Called by something far greater than the pain and suffering I saw around me, day after day, suicide after suicide. The next day I woke up before my husband and left our apartment. I took only a backpack full of food and water. I walked in the direction that the humming seemed the loudest. I walked for days, and then I saw them. Dozens of people dressed in dark robes, camped out in the middle of a forest. They had vans, trucks, a helicopter. They were hunched over maps. Drawing plans. When they saw me, they smiled. They knew about me already."

"The Source told them." Norman was staring at his wrists now, too, although he didn't have any visible scars.

"That's right," Maria said, looking up. "It was the Source. The Source was everything. It had called me to do its bidding, and its bidding was for all the world's dead to be collected and brought to it. I knew collecting corpses was a weird thing to do, but when you hear that humming, I mean really *hear* it, everything makes sense. Everything makes perfect sense, and with every corpse you collect, the better you feel. The more *right* you feel. Billions of people all over the globe may have been suffering, but that suffering was necessary. Suffering was only a stepping-stone to a greater, higher good. A step towards the Source."

Norman rubbed his temples. "So you went with them. You helped them."

"I did, and it was wonderful. It was like being on drugs. Really, really good drugs that never ended. Every time we sent another body onward our hearts lifted and—"

"It was like light, water, and God combined."

Maria grabbed Norman's hand. "How did you know that?"

"I've heard other Collectors talk about it."

"Oh," Maria said, releasing his hand.

"How did you come out of it?"

"What?"

"What made you stop . . . collecting?"

Maria stopped smiling. "It was stupid. One day I wasn't looking where I was going and I tripped and hit my head on a rock. When I woke up, the humming was gone, and so were the other Collectors. They left me alone outside a small town. They must have known as soon as it happened that I wasn't going to be like them anymore. The Source must have told them."

"Just like that, it was gone?"

Maria nodded and looked down at her wrists. "Yep. Just like that. But sometimes I think I can still hear it, you know. In the middle of the night, when I wake up and lie still. I can almost hear it then, but it's muffled. Farther away."

"Did you ever see the Source for yourself?"

Maria shook her head. "No, I was too new. Only the veteran

Collectors ever saw it. I only helped carry bodies to removal points. I never saw where they were taken."

"That's probably a good thing."

"I guess. I wonder what it would have been like to meet the Source. To see if it was as glorious as everyone claimed. I can still remember how beautiful that humming went, what it was like to be filled with water, light, and God. You'll see, Norman. If you make it far enough, you'll see."

After a muted good-night, Maria left his bedroom and Norman tossed in his enormous bed. The wine made him sweat into his pillow as his thoughts circled around what lay ahead. Eventually he got sick of trying to sleep and dressed in the dark. He left his bedroom and started down the complex hallways, recalling his way to the dining hall.

The dining hall's industrial-size kitchen was empty and lit by soft blue emergency lighting. Norman searched a freezer's wrapped and well-labeled contents until he found a package of bacon. He opened a few cupboards, banged some pans around, and started frying half a dozen strips of bacon on one of the electric stoves.

"Midnight snack?"

Dr. Briggs shuffled into the kitchen, dressed in a gray terry-cloth robe too big for his small frame. The scientist smiled and sat down at the kitchen counter beside the stove.

"Hey, Doc," Norman said, turning back to the bacon. "Couldn't sleep, either?"

"No. But I sleep very rarely, even when I am not busy with work or community affairs."

Norman found a fork and pulled the bacon apart. Each strip was thick with fat.

"Maria used to be a Collector," Norman said. "Why didn't you tell me?"

Dr. Briggs shifted in his chair. "Maria's past is her own business. I decided she would tell you in her own time, when she thought it proper. Does knowing her past change the person you know now?"

Norman stared at the sizzling bacon and imagined dark robes sweeping across green lawns. Those empty eyes. If she hadn't hit her head on a rock, Maria might have been one of the Collectors inside their house. Trying to take Jordan away from him.

"Norman, there are some things you still don't understand."

Dr. Briggs was standing by Norman's side now, leaning on his cane as he watched the bacon, too. The bacon was sizzling now, tiny burps of grease flying into the air. Norman turned the heat down a notch.

"Who do you think the Collectors are, Norman?"

"A bunch of lunatics who worship death. Necrophilia freaks."

"Not exactly. The Collectors are not a religious cult. The seppuku practitioners you say you encountered in Utah were a cult, indeed, but not so with the Collectors. A cult requires separate sentient beings worshipping a commonly perceived deity. The Collectors don't really worship the Source. They literally are the Source."

Norman flipped the bacon slices over. "How's that?"

"To begin with, each of them shares a common experience that I believe opened them to the Source."

"Which is?"

"Attempted suicide." Dr. Briggs tapped his cane on the floor. "The Collectors are failed suicides, Norman."

Norman pulled out two plates and two glasses from the cupboard and poured each of them a glass of cold water. The meaty, sodium smell of bacon hung in the air, pushing back the complex's general antiseptic scent. Dr. Briggs took his glass of water and sat back down at the kitchen counter.

"I believe each one of the Collectors, like Maria, has tried to kill themselves and failed in some way," Dr. Briggs continued. "Maria herself verified this. I believe this violent, physical action somehow triggered a very real physiological response in each Collector's mind. Who knows? Maybe this humming they speak of is only a few neuron modifications away from each of us. Think of the human mind as a radio, tuning through all the static until it fixes on a clear station. The Collectors have tuned into a powerful new station we can't fully hear yet."

The bacon was cooked. Norman speared the pieces and divvied them up. He turned off the stove and sat down beside Briggs at the kitchen counter.

"So what happened to Maria? She says she hit her head on a rock and lost the Collectors' signal. Is that really possible?"

Dr. Briggs bit a piece of bacon and chewed it. "I admit, her explanation sounds strange on the surface, but maybe that concussion truly did wake her up. Cleared her mind, so to speak. But I don't know if that's all of it, though. I think perhaps a part of her rebelled at collecting the dead in such a grotesque manner and fought the Source all along. Hitting her head could have been a subconscious excuse to block out the humming, to ignore its call. People are often much stronger than they think. After all, five years of this vile Despair and we're still here, aren't we? We're still talking in this kitchen. Eating good bacon."

"If the Collectors are failed suicides, why don't they try to kill themselves again and finish the job?"

"I'd imagine the Source doesn't want them dead, yet. The Source wants them to act out its own will. Like puppets."

Norman licked his fingers. "So, what do you think the Source is?"

"Something very, very wrong in the world."

Norman snorted. "Is that your scientific answer?"

"My friend, I don't think science has anything to do with the Despair. Nothing much at all."

They finished eating their bacon in silence. Norman thought about failed suicides. The scars on Maria's wrists. The Collectors preyed on those who'd succeeded where they had failed. How sad was that? How strange?

"Do you think God has anything to do with all this?" Norman asked. "I mean, do you think God has anything to do with the Despair?"

Dr. Briggs rubbed his round chin. "I hope God has nothing to do with all this. I hope God is asleep somewhere, dreaming of other things. Because if God is awake, watching us and willfully allowing this Despair, surely God must be a mad soul, a raving beast who needs to be put down immediately and without hesitation."

Norman wiped his hands on a paper towel.

"Amen, brother."

A few hours later Norman knocked on Maria's door. She opened it, already dressed for the day in khaki pants and a green blouse.

"Hi. Thought I'd stop and say good-bye."

Maria blew a puff of air up into her red bangs. "Really? You're not worried I'll try to steal your soul or something?"

"No."

Maria laughed, though Norman hadn't said it as a joke. She tilted her head and looked him over. "You haven't slept at all, have you?"

"Not really."

Maria closed the door behind her and stepped out into the hall. "Me either. Can I come and see you off?"

"Sure."

They started down the hall. He reached out and took her hand. He squeezed, and she squeezed back. Only five in the morning and the complex still slept. They walked its dim halls alone, like young lovers strolling through a park on a summer night.

"You know, sometimes it feels we're all stuck in some sort of purgatory," Maria said. "Everyone else has moved on. They've died, gone to heaven, been reincarnated as a chipmunk, returned to random particles of energy, whatever. What's left for the living? What do we do now? Walk around for fifty years, crying our eyes out until we die, too? That doesn't sound much fun to me. That sounds worse than being dead."

"Well," Norman said, "we can still hold hands."

A few minutes later Norman stood in a cool white room wearing only socks and a pair of navy blue briefs. Dr. Briggs and Maria hovered around him, examining the four small grenades they'd taped to his inner thighs.

"Are they hidden enough? He should look as natural as possible."

"If I had more time, I could create a smaller bomb."

Norman rubbed his arms. "Can I put my clothes back on yet? It's cold in here."

"Just a minute, Norman," Dr. Briggs said. "Maria, test those grenades one more time. Are they secure? We don't want one falling out while they're moving his body."

Maria tugged each grenade.

"Nothing's going to fall out here."

Dr. Briggs tapped the floor with his cane. "Good. Okay, Norman, you can put your clothes on."

"Thanks."

Norman put on a pair of long underwear, baggy cargo pants, and a leather belt. Next came a thermal undershirt, a fleece sweatshirt, and a winter coat. He slipped on a pair of thick wool socks and hiking boots. He zipped gloves and a stocking cap into the pockets of his winter coat.

"You look sharp," Maria said, putting an arm around his waist. "Like a secret agent."

Dr. Briggs pulled out a plastic bag from his coat pocket. "Nutritional vitamins, Norman. Take them every eight hours. They'll keep you going for a week without food, and better yet, they're pretty good at convincing your stomach that it isn't hungry."

Norman took the plastic bag and stuffed it in his coat pocket. "The perfect diet pills, huh?"

Dr. Briggs frowned. "Well, after prolonged usage they do have some unfortunate side effects. One's hair begins to fall out, one urinates blood, et cetera. . . ."

Norman laughed as something close to vomit rose in his throat. "Hair loss is the least of my worries now, I'd say. Hell, I wouldn't mind being around long enough to lose my hair."

Dr. Briggs nodded without smiling and left the room. Norman lay down on the canvas cot in the corner of the room, staring at the toes of his boots as Maria slid a pillow under his head. He had never paid much attention to his toes before, appreciated how each toe curled perfectly inside a shoe. He wiggled them now, savored the warm, scratchy feeling of wool. Maria covered him with a blanket and knelt beside him. Her hair smelled like Ivory soap and she kissed his cheek softly.

"You're a good guy, Norman."

"Thanks. You smell good."

Maria smiled and kissed his cheek again. Dr. Briggs popped back into the room carrying a white coffee mug.

"Norman, our team is assembled and waiting to transport you." Dr. Briggs handed Norman the mug. "You'll need to drink it all for it to take full effect. Remember, the drug is quite strong. You could be out forty-eight hours or longer. Your vital signs will be virtually nonexistent as your body slips into a comalike state. You will draw breath only once every two minutes."

Norman peered into the mug. The liquid was dark, like coffee or black tea. The question was, what did virtual death taste like?

"To review: Once you're under, our team will transport your body to downtown Seattle. The Collectors will find you lying in the rubble, apparently killed by smoke inhalation."

Norman put the coffee mug under his nose. He couldn't smell anything.

"The ship should take you back to the Collectors' base. Once there, you must penetrate its center, whatever that appears to be, and then—"

"Blow it up."

Dr. Briggs tapped the floor with his cane. "Correct."

"Right." Norman drank from the mug before he could think more about it. The scientist's potion tasted like black licorice gone rancid. Norman gagged it down and handed the cup to Maria.

Dr. Briggs bent over him. "How do you feel?"

"Fine. Are you sure this stuff works? I don't think—"

Norman's tongue thickened. The urge to breathe slowed in his lungs, then crawled to a halt. His toes tingled. Numb. Maria wrapped her arms around him. She was warm. "Good luck, Norman," a voice said, far off somewhere.

22

Darkness all around. Muck poured into his mouth, nose, and ears. He couldn't move. It was like being stuck in rush-hour traffic (back when there had been a rush, back when there had been traffic). Like quicksand. Like a firm hand on his chest, pressing against his lungs as he tried to breathe through the muck.

Where had all the oxygen gone? Was he dead?

If this was death, they could have it.

Something moved. A slithering eel.

No.

It was his hand. His hand was moving. He could feel it, there at the end of his arm. If he tried hard enough, he could make his other hand move, too, then both arms. He thrashed about, fighting the muck. Movement was the thing. If he could only keep moving, he could get somewhere.

Where?

Maybe it didn't matter. Anywhere was better than here.

Anywhere better than down in the muck. In this cold, oozing dark.

His hands felt for his face, missing wildly at first, only gradually nearing the grooves of his eyes, nose, mouth. Was this his face? Was this really what his face felt like? It felt too big, like a Halloween mask. Halloween, now there was a time of year, when the dark was scary and fun at the same time. Thrilling. You thrilled at the dark, at what could be lurking in your closet or beyond your porch light. The dark night was fun, and people cackled into the night, hurling candy and eggs and toilet paper.

But this dark was nothing like *that* dark.

This dark was much worse, and it tasted like ash. Nothing felt the same. Nothing was thrilling. This dark was like being dead.

But, wasn't that a light in the distance?

He rubbed his eyes. The glow remained far away, yet indisputable. It was bluish white. Beautiful. Something worth walking toward, so . . .

His legs trembled, straining at the sediment around his feet. The muck gripped his ankles and calves. Wrapped around him like an octopus, and he kicked until it let go a little, then he kicked some more. The light grew nearer, illuminating the murk like a torch and throwing shadows over the ocean floor. Tangled clouds of seaweed pulled back from the light. Pincer crabs scrambled in all directions as the light passed over them, and only the bottom-dwelling, eyeless fish swam on, noticing nothing.

His feet, which he had forgotten about, pulled free of the muck with a slurping sound. He was free, and the bluish white light was close now, shining on the ocean floor all around him, turning the mud beneath his feet as warm as beach sand. He could see the skeletal hulk of a Spanish galleon nearby, half-buried in the sand. Stingrays circled overhead like vultures, their pancake wings flapping noiselessly. A whale trudged along in the distance, its bristled mouth gaping as it drank up its lunch.

All these things were only background distractions, though, compared with the light. You didn't need to flinch. You could look right at it. It caressed you, wrapped its arms around you.

Angel?

Ghost?

He wanted to ask, but he didn't want to scare the light away. He wanted to keep it here with him forever. They would float through the ocean, the world, the whole universe, together. Nothing would keep them apart. They would not die, or falter. They would expand and grow and fill up the darkest corners, the smallest cracks in the cosmos.

But that wouldn't happen. Instead, the ground began to shake. Tremors. An earthquake. The crabs scuttled away across the ocean floor, fleeing in no particular direction. The sunken Spanish galleon rocked onto its side, a piece of its mast breaking off and floating away like a giant's ragged toothpick. Even the beautiful light trembled, turning a darker shade of whitish blue.

He wrapped his arms around the light. He wanted to comfort it. He would do anything for it, anything it asked. He would bring the light water when it was thirsty, and a blanket when it was cold.

Together they would thrive.

Luminous.

The ground continued to shake. The whale was long gone, the galleon was breaking apart, and the light was shaking like a frightened horse preparing to bolt. The light floated beyond his grasp. He tried to step forward, but his feet sank back into the mud. He flailed at the water, but he couldn't free himself a second time. The light drifted away, taking its luminosity with it.

Darkness sifted back around him, cold and hungry.

He wanted to explode.

He kicked and kicked and soon he was swimming, flying upward at a staggering velocity as the roof of the ocean approached. He spit bubbles as he went for broke. He burst through the water's surface, gasping. The air above was cold, and the sky an icy gray that made him wince.

This was nothing like the light he had known.

This wasn't even close.

23

Norman opened his eyes. The world came to him in a dim blur, then a slightly brighter blur. He felt his body swaying back and forth, as if he were resting in an immense cradle. His throat was dry and his tongue stuck to the roof of his mouth. Had he been drinking? No, this was no ordinary hangover. This couldn't even be an alcohol-poisoning-level hangover. Somehow glue had been injected into his muscles, his joints, and the marrow of his bones. The glue had dried, and now he couldn't sit up.

He willed his toes to wiggle. Nothing happened. He rested, tried to pull heat into his body, some kind of energy to get things moving. Pictured his toes lined up in a neat little row in his boots. They knew how to move. They wanted to move (or was he still dreaming? He was having problems breathing, with opening his lungs and pulling down air. Something was sitting on his chest, pushing the oxygen out of him.). Norman felt his toes move.

He rested again, imagining his entire body filling with electric sparks.

Neurons firing.

Blood rushing into deadened limbs.

Life.

Norman moaned. Good. This was good. He could move his tongue now, his shoulders. He could see a zipper in front of his face. Around the zipper, light showed through a transparent sort of fabric. A bag. Christ. He was in a body bag. The air was stale because he was in a body bag, on a shelf. Hard to breathe in a body bag, wasn't it? Norman slowed his thoughts and let the air come to him, let it filter slowly into his lungs. The zipper would open only from the outside. He needed to break out of the bag.

Norman lay still and gathered his energy. He thought of the female Collector, the gray-eyed one who'd left him in Oregon pinned against the tree, convinced he'd die a long, exposed death. He let the anger sink into his blood and pool in his heart, then forced it all into one colossal shoulder roll. He rolled off the shelf and fell onto a hard floor several feet below. The body bag's zipper split open as colorful flares shot through his vision, and he wondered if he was going to pass out, or die. Instead, Norman remained conscious and felt blood flow painfully return to his body. He lay on the floor for a long time, until he was able to shake his arms and feel real warmth replace the numbness. He sat up and took a look around.

Norman was in an immense, fluorescent-lit room surrounded by lengthy rows of metal shelving. On the shelves were body bags in six-foot intervals. Each bag was filled with a lumpy, unseen figure. Beyond the shelves were more shelves, continuing for as far as Norman could see. The only empty spot was on the second-row shelf right beside him, where he had undoubtedly spent much of his coma.

"Hell," Norman croaked, finally recalling where he was and why. He leaned his head back and closed his eyes. He wanted to sleep again, but not here. He wiggled his toes some more. He lifted his right leg and dropped it back on the metal floor. The resulting pins and needles at least felt better than nothing, so he did the same thing with his left leg. He wanted to start walking soon, in case the body bags around him began moaning to be let out.

Norman checked his pockets. He still had the bag of food pills, and the grenades were still taped to his legs. Norman got to his feet and propped himself up on a metal shelf. He groaned and tried to bend his knees. It was as if he had become an old man overnight. He released his grip on the shelving and stood back. The ship rocked beneath him, but he didn't fall.

Another thing. He was supposed to remember something else.

The video scrambler. A small tube, the size and shape of a Chap Stick, was stuffed into his back pocket. He took it out now and popped off its cap. The scrambler, one of many interesting devices created during Briggs's tenure at the complex, would send out a signal that looped archived video feed from every camera in the ship, erasing any digital evidence of its new stowaway. If the Collectors checked in on the freight ship, they'd find nothing out of order. Norman could walk its decks freely, as unseen as a ghost.

Norman pushed the scrambler's button and put its cap back on. The device gave off a low whine, warming up, then beeped three times, acknowledging that it had begun its work. Norman stuffed the scrambler back into his pocket and began walking the long rows of stored body bags on his way to the deck's exit. He tried not to look at them, focusing his attention on the return of blood to his tingling limbs. If she was here at all, Zero would not be dead and stored among all these bodies. She would be alive, up above. Norman came to a staircase. Each step caused searing pain, all the way from his calves to the top of his spinal cord. It was like learning to walk again. Norman clutched at the railing as he dragged himself up three flights of stairs, cursing the boat as it rolled beneath him, threatening to pitch him over like a dog shaking off a flea. Had Lazarus felt this bad after his four-day shift in the grave?

When he reached the top deck, Norman sat down and took in his surroundings. The ferry appeared middle-aged, maybe thirty, thirty-five years. Its riveted hull was stainless steel silver, and its twin smokestacks emitted a steady white stream of water vapor. He saw no crew, no passengers. The ship appeared headed north by northwest. Beyond the ship, far in the distance, was a purple smudge of color. Alaska.

Norman got up and began searching for Zero. He started

on the ship's top deck, slowly winding his way through the viewing gallery before descending a deck to the engine room and the several maintenance/junk rooms that surrounded it. He revisited the ferry's storage deck and its maze of shelves and body bags. He didn't open the bags, which would have taken days, but instead walked the rows shouting, announcing his presence to anyone still alive. He got no response and found nothing that indicated life. He returned to the top deck and checked beneath the tarps covering each lifeboat. He shouted at the empty deck, at the sea. No response.

He went back to the viewing gallery at the front of the ship. This time as he circled the gallery and its rows of plastic bucket seats, Norman noticed a locked door with a digital keypad. Interesting. He reached inside his coat and pulled out a small plastic card, another tool brought into existence by American tax dollars. According to Dr. Briggs, the card provided a type of electronic feedback that caused keypads to think the proper code had been entered. Norman held the skeleton key over the door's keypad. Nothing happened. Norman pressed the card closer, rubbing it against the keypad's silicon buttons. What if the card's batteries didn't work anymore? Did it even have batteries?

"C'mon, c'mon."

The lock clicked. Norman turned the knob and pulled the door open. A stench like spoiled meat mixed with piss and shit rushed out. Norman took a deep breath and ducked through the doorway. The room was weakly lit by one flickering fluorescent light. The windows had been painted black and covered with iron bars. Eight bunk beds lined the room's walls. Each bunk appeared to have someone sleeping in it, though no one moved or made a sound as Norman entered.

Norman went up to the first bunk bed and pulled the blanket back. The figure appeared to be a man about Norman's age. His face was swollen green and as soft as a rotted pumpkin. His hands were folded over his breast, as if when dying he'd prepared himself for a proper coffin burial.

"You've been dead awhile, haven't you, fella?"

Something shifted in another part of the room. "Hello?" Norman called out. "Someone here?"

Norman left the dead man and scanned the unmoving lumps on each bed. On a bottom bunk, at the end of the room, he found a pair of dark eyes staring back at him from above a ragged blanket. Norman knelt down beside the bed and exhaled.

"Oh, honey."

The figure stared back at him, unmoving. Norman touched the figure's knee through the blanket.

"Zero."

The staring figure lowered the blanket and he was able to see more of her face. For the first time in a long time Norman considered God's existence possible, if not necessarily desirable. All these miles and here was Zero, still alive.

"Thank you," Norman said. "Thank you."

She was much thinner now. Her cheeks were red and sunken, like an old-time consumption patient's. Norman cringed to see the deep hollow in her throat, the way she stared through him as if he were transparent. Norman shook her knee gently. "It's me, honey. Norman."

Zero blinked and focused on him.

Norman held out his arms. "It's okay. It's just me, Norman from Florida."

The girl reached for him. Norman pulled her out of the bed and pressed her against his chest. He stood up, cradling her in his arms as he started for the door. Five minutes ago, Norman would not have believed he possessed enough strength to carry so much as a branch, but the girl, the girl was too light.

The door slid open to the deck outside. A mercifully clean wind swept over them and carried away most of the hidden room's stench. Norman slid to the deck floor. He took off his long coat and wrapped it around the girl, who had closed her eyes and was shivering. Norman wanted to shout a stream of obscenities, but the words caught in his throat and he found himself simply staring across the ferry at a seagull that had landed on the deck railing. The seagull regarded him for a minute, as if Norman represented a new and interesting puzzle. Then the bird flapped its wings and took off, soaring back across the gray sea.

Norman found a small heated cabin that had once been a kitchen, probably used for concessions during the ferry's heyday. Norman woke Zero only briefly to give her one of Dr. Briggs's food pills and throw together a makeshift bed for her in the corner of the room, covering her again with his coat and cushioning her head with his gloves. The girl slept curled in a tight ball. She probably hadn't slept soundly for weeks, perhaps months. How long had it been since the attack? Most of summer? Hell. She was tougher than all of them. Made the Mayor look like a hothouse pansy.

Norman sat beside the girl and stretched. His body ached, his muscles exhausted after days of stasis. He kneaded his calves and thighs. Push-ups were impossible at the moment, but he was able to do a few knee bends before lying down again, his body quivering from the effort. The boat rocked beneath him and he dropped into a deep, blank sleep. When he woke up, he felt a little stronger and much sorer. Zero was still beside him, still curled into a ball. He lifted the jacket to look at her face. Her eyes twitched beneath her eyelids. Norman spoke her name and she whimpered back. He dropped the coat again and left the concessions galley.

Night had fallen. The ferry cut through the water without giving off any light at all. The navigational computer didn't need lights when it had radar, Norman supposed. He dug into his fleece sweatshirt's pockets and found the small, guitar-pick-sized flashlight that was also part of his spy gear. He clicked the flashlight on, and a wide beam of LED light leaped out across the ship's deck, much brighter than Norman had expected. He wandered the ship's deck until he found a ladder that led up to a small, elevated room. The metal rungs were damp and slippery, but he was able to pull himself up to a small hatch. He ran the skeleton key over the door's keypad. Something clicked, the hatch slid open, and he stepped into the electronic brains of the ship.

Norman sat down at the ship's computer console and situated himself. Dr. Briggs had prepped him for this moment by training him on a simulation program. Norman found now that the training was reliable, and if anything, the ship's navigational program was easier to manipulate than the sim. Within ten minutes, Norman had learned the ship's course and entered a few surprises of his own. He considered using the ship's radio to send a message to Dr. Briggs, but he decided it was too risky since he didn't know how closely the Collectors monitored the airwaves.

His work complete, Norman returned to the concessions galley to check on Zero. The girl was still wrapped up in his coat and snoring softly. Norman dug around the galley and found a pile of hand towels and clean aprons in a drawer. He dumped the fabric on top of Zero until it formed a cotton shell around the girl. He sat down and stretched. The grenades were still taped to his legs, and Norman was sick of their bulk, minimal as it was. He removed his pants and thermal underwear, gritting his teeth as he ripped off the medical strapping tape. Once he'd removed the grenades, he dressed again and checked each one over, making certain all the pins were still properly set.

Norman flinched as something tugged at his sleeve. Zero had woken up. Her brown eyes were less glassy than before, but this was still far from the cheery Zero he had known in Oregon.

"Well, hello there. Are you feeling any better?"

Zero tugged again at his sleeve. Norman pushed away the grenades and lay down beside her. She rested her head on his chest and he put his arm around her. "It must have been terrible, locked in that room like that. I'm amazed you survived, kid. You're very brave, you know that?"

Zero didn't respond. He was starting to see a pattern here. Was this shock? Norman had never been much for psychology, had barely passed it as an undergrad. If he had known how much of the world was going to revolve around it in a few years, maybe he would have studied harder. Learned more about depression, suicide, culture ennui. All that good stuff.

"After Oregon I went a little crazy, I think," Norman said. "Pops was dead and you'd been taken away. I walked the rest of the way to Seattle on foot, if you can believe that. It took weeks. And you know what? I saw this bear. It came right out into the middle of the highway and sat down in front of me. How do you like that? A big ol' grizzly, like he wanted to play patty-cake or something. I named him the King of Earth and then he lumbered away without so much as a paw swipe in my direction. I wish you could have seen that."

Zero had fallen asleep again. He could feel her breath on his cheek, her small chest rising and falling. Still alive. She was still alive. The ship's engines droned below them like a lullaby, and Norman watched the ceiling. When he was sure Zero was deeply asleep, he slipped out from under her arm and headed for the door. It was colder outside now, and Norman was glad Dr. Briggs had made him dress in layers. Norman stood at the ship's railing and watched the churning ocean. This dark blue water was much different from water on the coast of Florida. The whitecaps looked more like frosting than froth, the waves more frightening than enticing. How long would it take a person to become hypothermic in these northern waters? Ten seconds, twenty?

A massive wave came up, crested, and smacked against the ferry's lower deck.

The storage deck.

Pops could be stored down there along with the others, that placid, cloud-gazing expression still frozen on his face as he reclined on a metal shelf. Should he try to find him? Search every row, each body bag? What would the point be? To drag one more dead person from this floating tomb, to endure one more funeral while Zero lay shocked and broken already? Pops wouldn't have wanted Norman to go to the trouble. He would have told Norman to focus on the future, to worry about the girl and plan for their next move.

So Norman returned to the ferry's concessions galley, took one of Dr. Briggs's food pills, and lay down. The ship rocked beneath him. It was easy to imagine the high waves smacking the hull as it cut through all that cold water.

When Norman woke the next morning, Zero was sitting cross-legged beside him, studying one of the bombs, turning it in her hand as if examining an apple for brown spots.

"Those are dangerous, honey. You don't want to mess with them."

Zero shrugged and set the grenade on the floor, beside the others. She stood up and left the room. "Good morning, yourself," Norman said, grunting as he kicked off the blankets. His stomach was gurgling, so he took another food pill (somehow, it just wasn't the same as bacon and eggs) and drank from the galley's sink. He stashed the four grenades in a silverware drawer and went outside.

The wind had died off during the night. The ocean was calm. Zero leaned against the deck railing, and watching her, Norman recalled the long nights spent sleeping in the pickup truck, wild dogs howling in the distance as they all dreamed of Seattle. The memories might have come from fifty years ago, not earlier that summer. How could they have ever set their hopes so high? How could they have ignored the heavy hand of the Despair with so much evidence around them?

Norman joined Zero at the railing. A new, smaller blur had appeared on the horizon, a splotch of land on an otherwise empty sea. An island. Their island. The girl turned to Norman, her eyes red and lips gray.

"You made it to Seattle?"

"Yes."

"Did they have it? Did they have a Cure?"

"No. They didn't."

Zero leaned forward and considered the sea, her elbows resting on the ferry's cold metal railing. "Well, we'll be there soon enough, anyway."

PART FIVE

Borderland

24

In the brutal heyday of the Despair, Norman learned that a suicide survivor is not someone who has attempted to commit suicide and failed. You either commit suicide or go on living, however maimed you may be. A suicide survivor is anyone affected by the suicide of another person. The friends and family of a suicide. The abandoned children. The forsaken lovers.

He also learned that suicide lingered far beyond one person's death. Lingered beyond second-guessing, beyond guilt, beyond even grief. Once someone you loved killed himself, a new, dark trail of thought had been cut for you to follow. You could easily follow the trail through the densest patch of woods, the most twisted swampland, and if you left the trail, it still remained in the corner of your vision, always running parallel to whichever direction you were headed. Suicide survivors could, if they weren't careful, swiftly find themselves at the end of that freshly blazed trail, standing with one foot in life and one in death.

Norman called it Borderland.

The ferry's engines cut out, reversed, and cut again as it slid into one of the island's many docks. The ferry shuddered as it rubbed up against the dock's wall of rubber tires, and its foghorn blew loudly, announcing their arrival. Zero covered her ears with her hands and grimaced. They stood in the rear section of the cargo hold, deep in the maze of body bags.

The booming foghorn went silent. The ship swayed in the water. Zero lowered her hands and looked around at the stocked shelves. "I've never seen so many people before, and they're already dead. Isn't that pathetic?"

Norman shivered and blew into his gloves, concentrating on the warmth there.

"Do you think these are dead people from all over the world, Norman?"

"I don't know. Maybe they're all from Seattle."

Zero frowned. "What do you mean?"

Norman blew into his hands again. "Zero, I made it to Seattle, but the Collectors had already burned it to the ground. The only remaining citizens lived underground, in an old government complex. That's why I'm on this ship, actually. They planted me here. When we make landfall, I'm going to destroy the Collectors' headquarters. This has officially become a war."

"You're going to destroy it with four grenades?"

"They aren't regular grenades. They're called density grenades, and Dr. Briggs made them specifically for this trip. One of these suckers could level an entire city."

"Oh." Zero bent her knees, squatting inches above the floor with her arms crossed over her chest. "Pops is dead, isn't he?"

"Yes. He is."

Zero slowly rocked back and forth on her heels. "I saw him die, you know. I saw him go flying when the helicopter shot us. His arms were flapping but they didn't do anything, like he was a baby bird that couldn't fly."

Norman bowed his head.

"Maybe he's on this boat, Norman. Did you think of that? Maybe Pops is lying on one of these shelves right now. And what about my dad? He could be on this ship, too. A lot of dead people on board, right? Maybe I can find them—"

Zero stood up.

Norman grabbed her by the coat collar. "Don't even think about it."

"Let me go!"

"They'll be boarding any second. Stop it."

The deck's metal floor vibrated as something big rolled on board the ferry.

"You hear that, Zero? They're here."

"I don't care!"

Zero slipped off Norman's coat and bolted down the aisle. Norman put the coat on and went after her. He found the girl three rows over, kneeling above one of the bottom shelves and trying to unzip a body bag. Her dark hair hung over her face, and her hands shook as she fumbled with the zipper.

"Need some help?"

"Stay away from me, jerk."

"Okay."

Norman stopped where he was and peered down the aisle past Zero. They'd be here soon.

"Zipper stuck?"

Zero puffed out her cheeks, her forehead creasing as she worked on the body bag. A flap of cloth had gotten into the zipper's teeth, and it wasn't going to unzip anytime soon.

"Keep away from me, Norman. If Dad's down here, I'm going to find him."

Zero gave up on the body bag and crouched over another. This time the bag opened easily, releasing a ripe smell despite the frigid atmosphere. Norman looked over Zero's shoulder and saw a middle-aged woman, slightly bloated and eggplant colored.

Zero shook her head and zipped the bag up. "Not Dad."

Zero stood up and started for the next shelf. Norman lunged and knocked the girl to the ground. She clawed at his face, but he grabbed her wrists before she could do any real damage.

"I'll scream."

"No, you won't. Not unless you want the Collectors to lock you up again."

The girl followed his gaze far down the aisle to where dark shapes flitted about, pulling bag after bag off the shelves.

Norman let go of the girl. She understood the danger now, that there wasn't any time for craziness. In fact, Norman could hear human voices speaking nearby, in the next aisle over. The net was closing—

An alarm sounded above their heads, blaring much louder than necessary. Norman peered through the shelf and saw several dark robes sprint toward the ferry's stairwell. "Let's go, Zero. It's time."

They ran toward the cargo hold's exit. The braying ship's alarm stopped in midblare as they came to the end of the shelves. Three forklifts, their operator seats empty and engines still idling, were parked near the ferry's exit ramp. Norman and Zero stopped and looked around for any surprises.

"Guess even the Collectors need some help," Norman said, nodding at the forklifts. "So much heavy lifting, you know. Hard on the back."

The ferry's engines rumbled to life and the ship suddenly surged forward, pulling at the docking restraints. Zero fell onto her hands and knees. Norman lifted the girl up and they ran forward. The ferry shuddered with increasing violence, churning the water around it. Metal squealed against metal. Ropes whipped through the air as the loading ramp tore away from the dock. Norman tossed Zero across the gap and leaped after her. He landed hard and lay gasping on the dock as the ferry drifted away, its foghorn blaring as it headed back out to sea. He counted nine dark figures on the ferry's top deck, unmoving as they watched the island draw away.

"You okay?"

"Think so."

They helped each other up and surveyed the island's shoreline. Aluminum docks ran as far as they could see in each direction, some with ships docked and some without. At the end of each dock began a silver line of railroad tracks. These tracks ran all the way into the ash-gray mountains that hid the island's interior. Dark-cloaked specks and larger, forklift-shaped specks moved across the landscape. Transporting bodies, no doubt. Tossing them into the cattle cars until they piled high, all the way to the ceiling, before they sent the trains on down the line.

Zero turned back to the ocean. The ship had grown small and dark against the gray backdrop.

"Where do you think the ferry's taking them, Norman?"

"I told the ship's computer to go all the way to the north pole. Then I destroyed its keyboard."

"Good." Zero slapped the dust off her front. Norman gave the girl his winter coat back, noticing as she put it on that it hung down to her knees and made her look even younger than she was. Norman looked out at the ferry one last time. The Collectors still watched them from beneath the curtain of their hoods. Where they angry? Resigned to their defeat? Did they feel anything at all?

"Okay," Norman said. "Let's keep moving."

They walked slowly down the dock, which had twisted during the ferry's struggles and threatened to drop into the frigid water below. At the end of the dock sat six empty box-cars and two train engines, one on each end. Norman peered into the boxcars as they passed, making sure nothing was hiding from them. They could try to hijack the train and ride it to wherever the tracks went, but Norman didn't like this idea much. The other Collectors were bound to figure out what had happened, and once they did, all they'd need to do was locate the stolen train and send out an attack helicopter to destroy it.

As always, they'd be better off on foot.

Norman trudged through the sand, leading the way to a set of railroad tracks west of their own set. They walked along this alternative set of tracks, and before long they entered the mountains. Artificial canyon walls rose up around them, their steep sides so smooth they resembled opaque glass. A crack of blue sky could be seen overhead, and a chilly, ever-present wind blew through the canyon.

Norman walked on the gravel alongside the railroad, but Zero stepped directly on the rails. She hiked with her head down, her eyes focused on the railroad ties beneath her as if she were hell-bent on never missing a step. The rails themselves were polished silver from use. Nothing green spouted along the rails, or between the wooden ties. No sign of wildlife anywhere.

Zero stopped. "I bet this railroad goes to their hideout. Dark-robe central. And I bet their hideout looks a lot like hell. With fire and brimstone and dead people roasting on spits. They probably have a great Flaming Eye watching over everything, like in *Lord of the Rings*. They'll have machine guns and flak jackets and infrared goggles. They'll have tanks, and more helicopters. They'll have TV."

Norman scratched his chin. "Maybe, but we have the tricky element of surprise, and you can never underestimate the element of surprise. Haven't you ever heard of the Trojan Horse?"

They hiked on. Norman was tired, and he knew Zero was even more tired, but they had to put distance between themselves and the site of their little mutiny. He imagined the ferry roaring across the ocean, seeking its own destruction before the Collectors finally managed to shut it down. Funny how noble a machine could be with the correct programming.

Sunlight peeked into the canyon. They stopped to rest against a rock and drank from a water bottle they'd scrounged from the concessions galley. They each took a food pill and closed their eyes, soaking up the weak northern light. Red drifted through Norman's eyelids. A semitruck drifted across his mind, a horse, a feisty marlin. He felt as if he could sleep for centuries. He would wake up still at the bottom of this railroad canyon with the longest gray beard in the world, and the Despair would be ancient history, just another strange, psychotic blip in the history of humanity.

"When I woke up, I was in the back of a van," Zero said. "At first I couldn't remember what had happened. All I knew was that my ears were ringing and my arms and face were all scraped up. I tried to ask the Collectors sitting up front, but they wouldn't talk to me. They had me strapped down, like a wild animal. I remembered what had happened after a while and I started crying. They didn't look at me when I started shouting about Pops, about how they had killed him and maybe you. When we finally stopped driving, they made me march onto the ferry and up to the top deck, to the room where you found me. There were a bunch of people in the room already and it smelled like sweat and pee. The heat was turned way up, and even the women weren't wearing shirts, just bras. The Collectors told us the ferry was full now and that it was about to go back to where it belonged. They brought in a stack of food and water, then gave us each a bottle of pills."

Zero opened her eyes and squinted at the sky. "The first night on the ship two people took the pills without telling anybody. One of them was a girl my age, from Montana. After that first morning, when we found the first suicides, the others started to slip, too. I could see it happening in their eyes. I told them about you, Norman, about how you'd stood up to the Collectors and killed one of them, but nobody believed me. They all thought I was crazy.

"I got scared to sleep at night. When I woke up, maybe someone else would be dead. The first suicides were starting to smell, and the smell made it worse for everyone. We tried to break down the door, but it was too strong. People prayed and cried a lot, but nothing helped. Eventually, I was the only one left alive.

"I tucked the bodies into bed and put blankets over them, but their smell was still disgusting. I got used to it, though, and kept eating the dried meat and canned nuts they had left us. When I tried to sleep, I kept hearing something moving, thought I heard one of the dead people getting out of bed. I thought for sure I'd wake up one night with them standing over me, their purple faces falling apart in chunks."

Zero shivered, and Norman noticed the sun had dropped below the canyon walls.

"But I didn't take their pills. I knew you'd come for me, Norman. I knew you wouldn't stop unless you were dead. So I tried to keep drinking water and eating, and then you showed up. Like a knight in shining armor."

Zero leaned over and kissed Norman on the cheek.

"So thank you."

Norman sighed and stood up. His legs were sore, as if he had run a goddamned marathon. He didn't want to walk anymore. He was tired of walking. Traveling. He wanted to go home. He wanted to be back in Florida, swinging in a hammock with a drink in his hand.

"Zero, it was pure luck I found you. Sure, I hoped you might be on board, but I really came here to destroy the Collectors' base."

Zero took his hand and gave it a pat. "I know you don't like the fact that you're a hero, Norman, but you're just going to have to get used to it."

The farther they went, the more Norman could feel his feet blistering in the new hiking boots, fresh blisters forming on top of old blisters. The wind's intensity rose and fell, but it constantly howled on the edge of every thought, every sentence, every crunch of gravel underfoot. It was a murky afternoon that reminded Norman of gloaming, though he could no longer recall where he'd heard the word or what exactly it meant. He had trouble remembering a lot of things now, such as what it felt like to be warm, or the taste of real food. Dr. Briggs's pills might fool his stomach, but he missed actually tasting something, sinking his teeth into something.

Gloaming.

Gloaming gloaming gloaming.

Wait. What was gloaming? Had he read about it in the paper? Was it a type of depression? Was it like walking forever, toward nothing? Was a gloaming like a thick blanket of fog wrapped around your soul? Maybe he needed more vitamins. Maybe he needed to stop thinking about gloaming. Gloaming gloaming gloam—

"Do you hear that?"

Norman stopped. Zero was looking at him with her head cocked to the side.

"No," Norman said. "What?"

. . . *whump whump whump whump whump* . . .

Norman looked up at the crack of sky overhead. Wide enough for a helicopter to see them walking the tracks, but maybe—

"Zero, let's stand over there."

They ran to the canyon wall on their left and pressed their bodies flat against it. The higher the artificial wall went, the more inward it sloped, like an ocean wave. It would cover them. Probably.

The whumping sound grew louder. Norman stared across the tracks at the opposite canyon wall. Had someone actually been able to blast it this smooth? He couldn't see a single crack in the rock, as if a gigantic worm had single-mindedly burrowed through the mountain on its way to the sea.

"The bats, Norman. It's the bats again."

"Keep yourself flat. Pretend you're invisible."

The sky darkened and helicopter noise filled the canyon, waves of clattering sound bouncing from wall to wall as if an entire squadron hovered above them, waiting to launch a barrage of missiles. Norman clenched his fists and imagined punching a faceless figure in a dark, hooded cloak. He would start off with a left jab or two, maybe work the ribs, then he'd go for a right hook. One. Two. Then one more jab, setting the cloaked figure up for one huge, devastating uppercut. The figure would be surprised at his fury, his rage. It would stagger backward, its eyes wild, unfocused, then it would crumple onto the railroad.

The sunlight returned and the sound of helicopters receded. They waited a few minutes before continuing down the tracks. Norman kept looking over his shoulder, but the tracks behind them remained empty of trains and anything else. They came to the entrance of a tunnel as night fell.

"I don't want to go into that tunnel tonight," Zero said, sitting down.

"Me, too. Let's camp here tonight."

"Dinnertime?"

"Sure."

Norman searched his pockets and pulled out the bag of food pills and the water bottle. They downed the pills with their dwindling supply of water.

Zero sighed. "Nothing like home cooking, huh?"

Norman nodded. Was that mold he smelled coming from inside the tunnel? "You know, I don't like that smell."

Zero nibbled on her fingernails. "Dead people, you think?"

"No." Norman frowned. "More like flowers. Like flowers wilting in a small, stuffy room."

"Okay, so probably no dead people," Zero said. "But what about bats? Tunnels always have bats in them, don't they? Hanging from the roof?"

"And trolls, too. We'll have to fight the trolls."

Zero laughed and swiped at Norman's knee. Norman pretended to be hurt and collapsed to the ground. It felt good to lie down.

"It's so cold here," Zero said, sitting beside Norman and plucking at her coat. "It's not like the cold in Kansas, either. Winter cold isn't as bad as this place. Here it feels like my bones have turned into icicles and they'll never melt again."

"Must be the wind. Sounds like it's trying to say something, doesn't it? Like it's trying to make words."

Zero waved her arms. "Noooor-maaaaan. Noooor-maaaaan."

"Yeah," Norman said. "That sounds about right."

25

The island Norman found himself trying to sleep on was weighted with death. He could feel it. He could smell it. He could hear his own bones clattering behind every movement he made, his skin itching in sympathetic decomposition. All night long it was easy to imagine all sorts of things crawling, slithering, and running toward them from the tunnel's depths, but his favorite waking nightmare was zombies. The idea of zombies had gained credibility since the Despair, and if there was ever a place a person could find them truly walking the earth, shambling slow and steady as they sought warm-blooded food, it was on this island. Right here, inside this tunnel, at this time of night. He'd be almost asleep and then hear something moan nearby, gruff and toneless. Yet by the time Norman was fully awake nothing was there, not one shambling member of the undead, blood dripping down its cheeks like barbecue sauce as it bared its aching teeth.

Norman peered out of the tunnel into the lesser darkness

outside. His hearing, which had been dialed up to an incredible sensitivity since sunset, picked up the air-slapping sound of rotor blades. The helicopter grew nearer and Norman waited with heavy eyes. He did not feel like waking Zero. She needed to sleep, to shrug off their narrow escape from the ferry and the day's long, cold walk. Whatever waited for them inside the tunnel and beyond would be a bigger ordeal, perhaps the final one of their lives, and both of them would need all the rest they could get. Let the Collectors wear themselves out hunting. Let them worry.

Light poured into the canyon outside their tunnel. Norman squinted and held an arm to his eyes. The chopper had a spotlight focused in an extremely narrow radius, one capable of peaking between the canyon walls as it swept across the railroad tracks. Could they really see anything from such a distance? Or was this light merely a decoy, something to distract Norman with while others snuck up on their position?

The spotlight traced through more swaths of darkness, found nothing, and went away again. Norman lay back down. He drifted in and out of sleep for the rest of the night, never quite hitting a comfort zone, never quite escaping the night's cold or vivid images of people he had once known, pale, rotting arms outstretched as they drifted toward him, demanding one more hug.

"I dreamt about helicopters last night," Zero said as they started down the tunnel, their way illuminated by Norman's small LED flashlight. "They flew really low, right outside our tunnel. They had these bright beams of light that ran across the railroad tracks. I think they were trying to find us."

"That actually happened."

"What?"

"You were pretty tired, so I let you sleep through it. They weren't going to find us, so why worry about it?"

Zero's face puckered. They had taken their morning food pills, but she still looked like crap. Norman imagined he looked much the same, probably worse. He had actually been in a drug-induced coma two days ago, after all, more than halfway to dead. That couldn't be good for one's physical appearance.

"Why do you think they're trying so hard to find us, Norman?"

Norman cracked his knuckles. The sound was louder than he expected, reverberating off the tunnel walls in supersaturated stereo.

"Same reason I'm looking for them, I guess. Revenge. By all accounts I'm the first person to ever kill a Collector. If you think about it, the last five years have been pretty easy for them. Everybody's been depressed, and depressed people don't put up much of a fight. But now I've set a precedent, an example. You don't have to put up with their grave robbing. You can shoot them instead. So maybe now others are going to start fighting back and they'll have to work a lot harder."

"So they want to kill you to set an example."

"Yep. Though I think the damage is already done, really."

Zero patted him on the back. "Good job."

Norman smiled. "Thanks. I guess."

The tunnel narrowed as they walked. Norman could almost feel the pressure above them as the mountain bore down on the tunnel, threatening to collapse their slight pocket of open space and bury them beneath tons of rock. He saw something scuttle on the edge of their light.

"Ugh," Zero said, stepping closer to Norman. An obese rat with a thick, ropy tail sniffed at them.

"Wow. Now that's a rat. Must be eating well down here."

"I guess."

They started to walk a little faster than before. They didn't see any more rats, but Norman thought he could hear them scuttling beyond the flashlight's radius. Did they think humans meant food? Rats were scavengers, weren't they? How far would they follow them—

The ground beneath their feet began to vibrate.

"Earthquake?"

"No," Norman said, dropping to the ground and putting an ear to the railroad track. "Train."

Norman stood back up and led Zero away from the tracks, toward the damp tunnel wall.

"But what about the rats?"

"If you see one, kick it. If you see another one, I'll kick it."

The approaching train rumbled closer. They watched the area around them carefully, kicking away any rocks that could make a good rat hideout. Norman clicked off the flashlight as the train's disembodied headlight appeared, flaming orange. The train was an old model, the kind with iron wheels, and as it rolled, sparks jumped up beneath it like swarms of fireflies. Norman and Zero flattened out against the tunnel wall. Norman's jaw buzzed from the noise as the front engine passed. Trailing the engine were dozens of boxcars. Some of the boxcars were half-open, yawning rectangles of black on black. In the flickering spark light Norman saw a shape fall out and land a few feet away. Zero didn't squeeze his hand so much as smash it in a surprisingly strong vise, her fingernails clawing into his skin. Thankfully nothing else flew out at them as the boxcar procession passed and disappeared into the north end of the tunnel, leaving behind a ringing silence in its wake.

Zero yanked his arm. "What was that, Norman? What fell out?"

A wet, smacking sound came from nearby. Norman gritted his teeth and clicked the flashlight back on. A woman's body. She was dressed in a sensible wool skirt and sweater, with a pearl necklace still pressed against the bloated skin around her neck. A small army of rats had already fallen upon the woman and were chewing on her plump calves, their small, sharp teeth tearing the skin away in thin, purple strips, as if her flesh had turned into bits of soggy wallpaper.

Zero screamed. Norman tugged the girl away from the corpse and started up the tunnel. "It's okay, honey, it's okay." Norman tried to keep his voice calm and even. The gloaming was still around, he realized. You just couldn't see it anymore, and maybe that was worse.

Zero started to retch, but nothing came out. No food in the girl's stomach, really, and they both verged on dehydration already. They had less than a third of the water bottle left, and there probably wouldn't be any clear mountain streams to drink from along the way. If the island wasn't totally dry, every ounce of its water was probably contaminated anyway.

Norman pulled Zero along. "That was perfectly natural," he found himself saying. "Perfectly natural. The cycle of life. The cycle of death. Nature in action. Animals feed on things to live, even plants feed on things to live. Those rats were hungry. Why not let them eat, too? That woman doesn't care what happened to her body, Zero. That woman is no longer with us. She's in heaven, if there is one, and if there isn't, she certainly isn't lingering anywhere near her old body. She's gone. Long gone."

Zero had stopped retching, but she still squeezed Norman's hand as if she were trying to crush it flat.

"I used to hate that people died, too," Norman said, looking at the girl. "But it started happening so much I got used to it. The Greeks said that every man was born owing a death, and they were right. My friends are dead. My parents are dead. My wife is dead."

Zero's chest hitched. "Your wife?"

"Yes, my wife."

"You loved her, didn't you?"

"Yes. Very much."

"Then why did you decide to live after she died?"

Light appeared ahead. "I thought about dying, but I guess back then I was too mad, too pissed off, to kill myself right away. I wanted to fight against something, to start a war. But I've done that now, and I really don't feel that much better. Nothing's brought Jordan back, and nothing will. My life will always be different now, but at least it will still be a life. I'm still here talking with my friend Zero. It's only been a few months, but I already wouldn't want to give up the memories I've had since Jordan's death."

The tunnel was coming to an end. The gray light was an opening, a perfectly round opening. Zero's hand loosened its grip.

Beyond the tunnel, the train tracks continued over a lengthy, windswept bridge and disappeared into another tunnel. On both sides of them bridges, all identical to their own, spanned the mountain gap like spokes running toward the same hub. Far below, the ground was a broad expanse of gray. Not ground, but a paved runway, Norman realized. Dozens of planes dotted the runway, taxiing toward takeoff as others landed.

"Airplanes," Zero said. "Those are airplanes, aren't they?"

Norman squinted. "The Collectors' air fleet, I guess. Don't worry. They can't see us."

"You sure about that?"

"No."

"Alright then," Zero said. "Let's not dawdle and make ourselves all obvious and stuff."

They started across the bridge. Norman watched each step carefully, going from wooden tie to wooden tie without thinking too much about the open space between. The gaps weren't wide enough to fall through, exactly, but you could easily wedge your foot into one, trip, and fall forward. Maybe the tracks would catch you, or maybe the wind would come along and sweep you away. The fall would be a hundred feet, easy, and then all that asphalt runway hurtling at you. . . .

Norman stopped and glanced back at Zero. She seemed less nervous than he was, lightly leaping from tie to tie like a ballerina.

When she noticed him watching her, she smiled and waved. "This is fun. I like bridges."

"Well, I'm glad you're enjoying yourself so much. Hell, maybe we should pretend this island is really only a strange amusement park. A cross between a haunted house and a roller-coaster ride."

Zero caught up to him. "Okay. How about we call it Death Island? That's a good amusement-park name, isn't it?"

Wind gusted, causing Norman to waver back on his heels. He cursed and continued forward. The bridge didn't sway underfoot, at least. It felt solid. It had to be, it bore the weight of a constant stream of freight trains. But what if a train came now, barreling out of the tunnel? Nowhere for them to hide, no pedestrian sidewalk to jump on. They'd have to drop and hang from the edge of the bridge, the whole thing shaking above them. Norman was already exhausted, how would he hold on to the railing? How would he pull himself back up once the train passed? Maybe it would be better if he jumped right now. All it would take was one long step, to the right or to the left. Norman put a foot out, testing the air.

"Norman!"

Suddenly he was lying face-first on the tracks, his lower lip puffing out as Zero pummeled his back.

"What do you think you're doing, you asshole?"

More punches. She had him pinned, her knees digging into his back. What had just happened?

"You have no right to do that," Zero shouted in his ear. "You have no right to leave me alone, damn it. What were you thinking? How stupid can you get? You fall off this bridge, you're a goner. You fucking hypocrite, a minute ago you said it was better to go on living!"

Humming. A humming up ahead. Not a gloaming at all, but a humming. He could hear it now, the sound of a billion bloodthirsty mosquitoes. But it had been there all along, hadn't it? Since Florida. Since Jordan. Since Thompson the Collector. The humming wanted him. His presence was required.

Zero smacked the back of Norman's head. Norman tried to push himself up, but he was too exhausted.

The girl shouted in his ear, "Where do you think you're going, Jumpy?"

"Let me up."

"Why? So you can finish jumping?"

Norman closed his eyes. How could he have missed it for so long? It wasn't really like mosquitoes at all. No. It wasn't anything like an insect. It was more like light, water, and God combined.

"I'm not going to jump, Zero. Let me up."

"Why should I believe you? A minute ago you were fine, but then you almost killed yourself. Just like my dad, you asshole. You're like my goddamned dad."

Norman winced. "I'm sorry. I didn't know what I was doing. It was like I was sleepwalking."

Zero's weight shifted slightly off him, but her knees continued to dig into the small of his back.

"Sleepwalking?"

"Like a ghost."

"A ghost, huh? Ladies and gentlemen, Norman has left the building."

She pressed a little harder, then got off his back. "Don't try that again, okay? I don't want you to be splattered all over the runway down there. You look much better unsplattered."

Norman took a deep breath, enjoying the full use of his lungs again. He got up and saw that they were halfway across the bridge.

He faced Zero. "Thanks for stopping me. I'm sorry."

"No problem," Zero said, her face flushed and eyes glistening. "I would have done the same thing for a friend."

The bridge creaked with the breeze.

"Can you hear that humming, Zero? In the distance?"

"Sure," she said, tilting her jaw. "I thought it was only in my head."

"No. I hear it, too. I think it's coming from up ahead, from inside the next tunnel."

"What do you think it is?"

"Nothing would really surprise me anymore. Do you want to turn back? You can if you want. I'll be okay."

Zero shook her head. "I've come this far, haven't I? Might as well see what's caused all this trouble while I'm here."

They crossed the bridge, and this time Norman ignored the humming as best he could while Zero talked steadily from behind him, reminding him to put one foot after the other, steady wins the race.

The rats in the next tunnel didn't bother to scuttle away when light fell on them. Some were so bloated their stomachs dragged on the ground as they waddled, their plump, pink tails dragging behind them like uncut umbilical cords. Norman listened for approaching trains, but you couldn't hear much above the humming that bounced off the uneven tunnel walls.

"What if the flashlight runs out? Then we'll be in the dark, won't we? With all these ugly rats."

Norman put an arm around Zero and pointed to his feet. "It's okay. These boots were made for rat kicking. Seriously. Look at those stiff toes."

Norman kept them moving at a fast march. The tunnel's end became visible up ahead. Not sunlight beyond it this time, though, only a deeper shade of black. The humming was louder now, with a pulsing, syrupy throb beneath it that caused his teeth to vibrate.

Here it was.

At last.

Norman handed Zero the flashlight and bolted forward, no longer concerned about conserving energy, no longer worried about anything. He had come a long way to see what was beyond this tunnel, calling to the world like an angry parent.

He sprinted into the dark.

26

Norman emerged from the tunnel at top speed but skidded to a stop almost immediately. In front of him was a wall of black with a center so dense it was almost blue. Behind him, Zero shouted for Norman to wait up, wait up.

The girl joined him and shone the flashlight into the darkness. They were standing on the edge of a sheer drop-off, at the edge of a darkness that appeared bottomless and hummed as if alive. The void seemed to gather darkness upon itself, collapsing inward like a black hole, and as you gazed into it, your eyes hungered for light, color, or any substance at all.

Zero kicked a rock over the cliff's edge. "So. What do we do now?"

Norman squatted on his heels. "We have the density grenades, but I don't think Dr. Briggs imagined anything like this. This doesn't look like some military compound we can blow up. This looks like something already blown-up."

They retreated to the tunnel's entrance and sat down on the last section of the railroad. This whole remaining strip of land resembled a mountain rim, Norman realized. If they walked far enough either way, they'd probably reach another tunnel's entrance, another set of rails. On Death Island, all roads led here.

To this pulsing, hypnotic emptiness.

"Norman."

Zero was shaking his shoulder.

"Yes?"

"I said, what do you think is down there?"

"I don't know."

"Whatever it is, I bet it's alive. Can you hear that? That's its heartbeat, I bet."

The rails vibrated beneath Norman's feet. He shuddered and bent over as a dull pain blossomed in his stomach. They still had a handful of food pills, but this wasn't hunger. This was sickness. This was like radioactive fallout, coming from the void itself.

"Train's coming," Zero said, looking down the tunnel.

He had to get up and get moving. Could he trust his feet, though? Once an object is put in motion, it tended to stay in motion, didn't it? What if he walked right off that cliff over there?

Zero stood up. "Let's go farther down, so they don't see us."

Norman allowed himself to be led away from the tunnel's entrance. "I think this is far enough," Zero said, stopping about fifty yards from the rails and clicking off the flashlight.

Reddish orange light appeared from within the tunnel as the train neared. The engine surged into view and screeched to a halt, throwing a wave of sparks into the darkness.

This engine also had several freight cars attached, many of which were out of sight, still inside the tunnel. A dozen Collectors emerged from the engine car, barely visible as they flitted to the first of the freight cars and opened it. They went to work forming a line and moving the bodies, pitching them over the void's edge as if they were nothing but more wood for the fire.

The Collectors delivered body after body to the void. Norman and Zero continued to watch, but after a while Norman's gaze slipped off into the darkness. The void was simply more interesting. He could feel it tugging at his mind constantly now. Chipping away.

"I think they're done," Zero said. Norman blinked and turned back to the train. The Collectors were stepping back into the engine car. Zero exhaled as the train, which must have had a second engine on its opposite end, slid back into the tunnel like a rectangular snake. Soon the train's light disappeared, and it was dark again.

"I'm glad they're gone," Zero said. "If I have to see one more dead person today, I think I'm going to scream."

Norman clicked the LED flashlight back on. He expected to be momentarily blinded, but now the light was dim, as weak as a night-light. Zero had bit her lip so hard it was starting to bleed, but she didn't seem to notice. Norman felt around his many zippered pockets and pulled out three of the grenades, saving one for Just in Case. The bombs felt reassuringly heavy in his hands, like metal oranges.

Zero frowned when she saw them. "Won't they bring down this whole mountain?"

"Maybe. If they do, we'll just start running really, really fast."

Zero folded her arms across her chest. "Very funny."

Norman fingered the pin on one of the bombs. Dr. Briggs had said to simply pull the pin, toss the grenade, and wait sixty seconds for the boom. He could handle that.

"Okay. Zero, get inside the tunnel."

"What about the rats?"

"They can't be as bad as three density grenades going off. I'll join you in a second."

Zero went off into the tunnel. Norman put the small, triangular flashlight between his teeth and pulled all three pins. He walked up to the void, gazed down, and hurled the grenades as far as he could. The bombs disappeared from sight as soon as they left his hand. He jogged back to the tunnel's entrance and crouched beside Zero, his knees popping.

One minute passed.

Two minutes.

And still, nothing happened.

Zero put her hand on his shoulder. "Norman?"

"I don't know."

They waited another minute before returning to the

tunnel's entrance. Beyond the tunnel the hum approached a new, angry crescendo. Norman ran his hands through his hair, hoping a deluge of blazing flame would appear from below, purifying everything, but the darkness remained and here he was: cold, hungry, and so damn heartbroken it surprised even him.

27

They peered back over the void's edge. Zero cocked her head to the side and her hair spilled off her shoulder, swaying over the void like the first strands of an unfinished rope.

"Remember back in Kansas, Norman? When you and Pops showed up at our house after my dad died?"

"Sure I do." Norman spat into the darkness.

"Margo and Herb thought you guys were Collectors, and at first it was sort of funny, like they were being dumb and everything, but I started thinking about it back on the ferry and it started to make sense. You guys were collectors, but a good type. The kind who help living people out and make them move when they need to move. Maybe Movers is a better name. They're Collectors, you're Movers."

Norman blew warm air into his hands and shifted from foot to foot. The temperature had dropped in the last few minutes.

"Some job of moving we did," he said. "Look where you've ended up."

"Well, things could be worse, you know. I could be like those wild girls who murdered Alice's twin sister in the street. I could be running around with a hatchet, chopping up people for sport."

"You wouldn't have turned out that way."

"You don't know that."

"Yes, I do. You're a good kid."

"We would have run out of food eventually. Margo and Herb would have died, one way or another. Who knows what I would have done. Maybe finish drinking all the booze in town, then shoot myself in the head? Who knows. It doesn't really matter. What mattered was that you guys showed up and offered me some hope. So, you know. Thank you."

"We were just—"

"Hey. For once shut up and let someone thank you, okay?"

Norman closed his mouth and nodded. He sat and dangled his legs over the cliff. One of his shoelaces had come untied, so he tied it. Zero sat down beside him. She swung her legs out and let them drop back quickly, the heels of her shoes thudding against the cliff wall.

"All this way, and we can't do anything."

"Well . . ."

"Well what?"

"We still have one grenade left."

"So?"

"So maybe the problem was in the delivery. Maybe the other bombs weren't delivered properly."

Zero stopped kicking her legs. "What do you mean?"

"I mean, the bombs might not have made it to the target. I threw them into the pit, but we don't know where the pit goes, or what deadening effect it might have. For all we know, those grenades might have landed miles away from whatever is making that noise."

"Norman," Zero said. "Stop."

"Am I wrong?"

"No, but—"

"So if I go down there, I'll be able to get closer. Maybe stuff the grenade down its throat, if it has a throat."

Zero put her face in her hands and spoke through her fingers. "But you'll die, Norman."

Norman leaned back and rested his weight on his palms. White clouds drifted across his mind. "Well, no plan is perfect."

Norman walked Zero to the tunnel's entrance. He gave her the remaining food pills and the electronic skeleton key, but she wouldn't take the flashlight from him.

"Nope. You take it. You'll need it more than me."

"What about the rats? The rats in the dark?"

Zero lifted up her right foot. "You see these tennis shoes? They're made for rat stomping."

Norman smiled and hugged the girl to his chest. "Stay on the rails, okay? It might be dark, but you'll be able to feel the rails under your feet and follow them back to the beach."

"I will. 'Bye, Norman. I love you."

They let go. The girl turned her back to him and entered the tunnel, stepping beyond the flashlight's range and disappearing into the darkness.

"Remember, this isn't suicide," Norman shouted into the mouth of the tunnel. "And stay on the rails!"

The cliff was filled with cracks large enough for Norman to wedge his fingers and toes into. He stuffed the flashlight into his pocket and found it shone through the fabric with just enough intensity to reveal the next foothold in the rock. He descended rapidly despite his fatigue, somehow propelled by the humming around him. After a long, dull stretch of nothing but climbing, Norman started talking aloud, as much to himself as the void.

"The Despair was worse for my wife than it was for me, you know. I really didn't have that many friends to lose in the first place. She had dozens. Hell, maybe a hundred. And they all loved her. Really, really loved her. The phone used to ring all the time, and she'd talk on it for hours. Helping people with their problems, I guess. I'd be studying for some exam or another, late into the night, and I would hear her talking about someone's cheating boyfriend, dying parent, or terrible job. It made me jealous, all those people relying on her. Asking Jordan's advice, taking little pieces of her away from me."

A draft of air swept up the cliff. Norman caught the smell of something nasty and tried not to imagine what it represented.

"After the Despair started, people stopped calling our house. To fill all this new free time Jordan started to paint in watercolors and drink green tea. She read books by Charles Dickens, lit scented candles, and took really long baths. I did my best to keep her happy. I told jokes, acted like animals, robots, anything to make her laugh. We read poetry together in bed. On the calendar holidays I cooked ten-course meals, complete with dessert and coffee. It wasn't enough, though. Death spreads. It creeps into your thoughts, your dreams, your sex life. It can make the food you eat taste like ash."

Norman's back burned and his fingers were growing stiff. How long had he been climbing? How much longer until he reached the bottom? A while, he guessed.

"I could use a drink, I'll tell you that. A long drink of whiskey, with ice cubes. Doesn't that sound good?"

No reply from the void. Just more steady, steady humming.

"You know why I was fishing that morning? Why I was gone? To tell you the truth, I wanted to get out of the house. We'd had a fight the night before, and I wanted to get out of the house and far away from my wife. I was sick of her. Sick of us. So I took off early, without saying good-bye, and went down to the river. I spent all morning fishing, with no idea at all something was wrong.

"That morning was the first sunny day after a week of rain. The woods on both sides of the river were two dozen shades of green, at least; dewdrops still gleamed on each blade of grass. The air smelled sweet, like honey and jasmine. The river was clear and running high. You could see fish all up and down it jumping up to the surface to snap at all the bugs and mosquitoes. A blue heron flew right past me, close enough to touch, and the other birds were all awake, too, chirping and singing like mad as the sun rose and broke above the trees, and I remember closing my eyes and listening to it all, breathing the spring morning into my lungs until my chest warmed and my muscles relaxed. Life was good, I decided. Good enough."

Norman coughed and reached for the next descending handhold.

"Well, I guess we all know how long that mood lasted, don't we?"

A falling pebble bounced off Norman's nose. He looked up and saw a patch of darkness descending upon him. He dug his fingers into the cliff as deeply as he could, bracing himself.

He saw one loose, flapping arm.

One pale face.

And then a heap of bodies, knocking him from the cliff and sending him plummeting along with everyone else.

28

Norman thought the fall had killed him, but this didn't seem like heaven. It was a lot more like Florida. It had palm trees like Florida, orchids like Florida, and the sun was hot like Florida. The sky was a strange shade of white, though, and the insects were humming much louder than they normally did.

Wait.

He was standing in the middle of a street, in the middle of a familiar town.

He was home.

Norman's hometown was as crumbled as he remembered it being, the homes around him either sagging inward or totally collapsed. Everything was green, too. From emerald to moss to pea green. If this was a dream, it was as vibrant and realistic as dreams could get, the sort of hyperdream Norman imagined veteran drug users might have. He could feel the shadowy slip from warm to cool as he passed beneath the rustling palm trees that lined the street. Deep, steaming puddles of murky water pocketed the sidewalks. Dead night crawlers lay prostrate everywhere, their thin strips of red flesh baking in the sun as the lizards tracked them down one by one. The air smelled like dirty rainwater, the pungent gutter kind that came from flooded sewage tanks and too much soggy heat.

Norman turned down a street and discovered his house waiting for him. The same chipped white paint, the same two stories, the same empty front porch. Next door Pops was absent from his own front porch, though the power generator the old man was working on sat beside his rocking chair. Norman surveyed the scene one more time, wary of a trap, then bolted for his front yard, pounding up the front porch steps with his arms

open

shouting for Jordan Jordan Jordan Jordan, wanting to lift her off her feet, her blond hair whipping around like a gold banner, and maybe this was heaven, maybe Norman had died and gone to heaven after all.

He turned the knob.

Pushed.

Stepped into his dim living room.

"Jordan?"

Norman ignored the dim first floor of his house and went upstairs. She was still sleeping. He'd surprise her. Wake her up. He was back home, and they'd have a party to celebrate. They'd drink wine and take off all their clothes and—

Someone had nailed boards across their bedroom door. Norman had a dim memory of hammering (some brief yet furious stint of home repair), but now the boards seemed unbelievably stupid. How would Jordan get out of their room? How could he get in?

Norman tore the boards away with his bare hands. They felt soggy and thin, like cardboard, and soon Norman had the whole mess cleared away. He knocked on their bedroom door.

"Jordan?"

The doorknob turned and Norman stepped inside. He smiled to see his wife sitting up in bed, propped up on pillows as she wrote in her journal.

"Good morning," Norman said. "I'm glad to see you're up."

"What are you writing about?" Norman asked, sitting at the foot of the bed. Jordan didn't look up.

"Hello?" Norman waved a hand in front of her eyes. His wife didn't blink. "Hell. I'm dead, aren't I?"

Jordan looked up from her journal, but not at him. She stared out the window, as if considering something important, and shut her journal. Her eyes were red from crying. Norman wondered if Jordan was crying because he was dead, because she was alone and he was dead. She reached for the bottle of pills by the bedside and Norman finally remembered.

"Don't touch those pills," he said, jumping up from the bed. "You don't need any more pills. You need to go outside, get some exercise and sunshine. You really don't need the pills."

Jordan twisted the bottle in her hands and popped off its cap.

"Sleeping pills? But it's still early. You don't want to sleep yet."

Their house began to hum loudly, as if the neighborhood insects had flown in through an open door and piled inside, filling the entire first floor with their glossy exoskeletons and quivering antennae. Jordan cocked her head, as if she could hear the humming, too, but continued with her business, pouring a large handful of white pills onto the palm of her hand.

Norman walked over to the window. Whether he was dead or not, Norman was definitely visiting the past. The past him was still down at the creek, fishing. Next door Pops had come outside and was busy working on the old generator on his front porch. Both of them were totally oblivious to what was happening in this stifling little room, to the town's third citizen.

Jordan picked up a glass of water. Norman ran toward her as she raised the pills to her mouth. He swatted at her hand and passed through it, a sharp spike of cold running up his arm. Jordan nibbled on the pills as if they were popcorn and popped several into her mouth.

"Spit those out! Goddamn it, spit that shit out!"

Jordan took a drink of water and swallowed. She got out of bed, passed by Norman without looking at him, and shut the drapes. She lay back in bed for a few more minutes, then took six, seven more pills. Norman cursed, paced, and thought about going to get his shotgun. Maybe he could shoot himself and avoid witnessing this.

Jordan closed her eyes, sighed, and opened them again. She took four more pills, for good measure.

Norman sat back down on the edge of the bed. Why was he here, watching this shit? It had been bad enough to find her in the first place, to fight over her body with the Collectors. By nightfall, this whole room would be covered in gluey blood and bone-flecked pulp.

Jordan pulled the white comforter over her face, so only her blond hair showed. Norman wanted to throw back the blankets and pound his wife's chest like a drum. Instead, he stayed at the edge of the bed and plugged his ears against the humming.

But it was useless.

It was all so damn useless.

———

The nightmare didn't end at that moment, as Norman expected it to, but continued. Jordan rolled onto her side and gave a small moan. Norman stood up and left the room, slamming the door behind him. He stomped downstairs, strode through the living room without opening the drapes, and told Jordan's collection of potted plants that they could go fuck themselves.

Outside, most of Norman's hometown had disappeared. All that remained was a small slab of sidewalk connecting his house to his neighbor's. Beyond this, where the street had once been, was a marshy swamp filled with pea green water, cypress trees, and several fat crocodiles bobbing on the water's surface, looking for lunch. Mosquitoes and gnats hovered over the water in dark, jittery clouds, and occasionally a fish would jump out of the water, gulping. Ruby-colored birds flitted through the air and called to each other in short, melodic bursts.

"Pretty sight, ain't it?"

Norman looked over to Pops' house. The old man sat on his front porch, wearing the same oil-stained overalls and wraparound sunglasses as always. Norman stepped forward.

"Pops. You're alive?"

Pops shook his head. "No, son. I'm not. But that doesn't mean you can't come over for a little chat, does it? One last town meeting?"

Norman walked to Pops' house, careful to stay on the sidewalk. The leafy, prickly vegetation beyond the sidewalk rustled ominously, and Norman half-expected a vine to lash out as he climbed the creaking porch steps. He sat down in a rocking chair beside the old man.

"Good to see you, Pops. I'm glad you can see and hear me, at least."

"Sure I can see you. You've lost weight."

"I'm sorry about the way they killed you. We shouldn't have been on the road after Utah. I should have guessed they'd be on our trail like that."

"It's okay, Norman. It wasn't your fault. And besides, I had a pretty good run."

"Am I dead, too?"

Pops glanced down at his stained hands. "Not yet."

The swamp beyond the porch railing was so damn vivid. How could this be a dream? This didn't feel like a dream.

"Where are we, Pops?"

"I don't know, really. I think of it like cracks in an old wooden floor. You've fallen through one of the cracks, and now you're talking to me."

Norman squinted into the strange light that hung about the swamp like a fog. "My real body is at the bottom of the void, isn't it? I'm lying there right now, with all the dead."

"Yes, that sounds about right."

"But what is it? What's down there with us?"

Pops scratched his arm and smacked his thick lips together, sucking his teeth as he thought over the question. Norman tried to see the old man's eyes, but the wraparound shades hid them well. Probably a good thing, Norman decided.

Pops spit something wet and brown onto the porch floor. "Sorry, son. I can't say what it is, exactly, and I don't think it really even matters. All I know is that the Source is real, a physical thing in a physical reality. The Despair didn't appear out of thin air, you know. It started when the Source began to send out a signal that intensified our worst fears. Our pain, our loneliness, our worry, all those times we wake up at three a.m., sweating and wondering if we've screamed out loud. The Source took all that and played it like a goddamned drum. Some folks have managed to ignore its summons so far, and some have heard it in a different way, but if it keeps calling, soon every last living person will have to answer."

Norman put his head between his knees. The humming was still in the background. A constant, thirsting sound. Why had he never appreciated silence before? How calm and soothing it was?

Pops fell quiet, as if he could read Norman's mind. They rocked and listened to the swamp. This could be eternity right here, Norman thought. Sitting, rocking, and whittling wood. Listening to the birds chirp, the bugs drone. They could talk about minute differences in the weather, and if the weather never changed, they'd pretend it did, anyway. Pops was a good guy, and sitting here reminded Norman of how much he missed the old man. Life was an endless cycle of saying good-bye to people you loved, of losing people who mattered to you. The Despair had cut through humanity's families, communities, and countries like wildfire, speeding up this endless process of loss. Now almost everyone was gone, and the only people remaining had little to look forward to, a hard life of survival as the world they had once known crumbled around them for the rest of their lives, constantly reminding them of their loss, their civilization's defeat. Sure, they could rebuild it all; the question remained if they would want to. Would they find the heart to go on? Perhaps humanity would quietly die now, slowly burn out like the orange embers of a campfire.

Pops glanced over at Norman. "The Source put on a show for you, didn't it? Took some wind out of your sails?"

"Yep. It showed me the day Jordan killed herself. Let me watch her swallow the pills and everything. I couldn't do anything but stand there and shout. I couldn't even touch her."

Pops folded his arms across his chest. "Same thing happened to me when I first came here. Showed me my Helen. How she climbed all the way up the town's water tower, how her arms trembled as she pulled herself up each rung, and how she wet herself as she slipped off. I tried to run under and catch her, but she fell through me like a cold wind."

A snowy egret flew across the swamp and disappeared into a grove of mango trees. "Jordan loved you," Pops said, looking at Norman. "You know that, don't you? Her killing herself had nothing to do with you. She decided to move on, that's all. Like a lot of other people we knew."

"Yeah," Norman said. "I know."

"Good."

Pops coughed and spat a clump of something pink and

slimy over the porch railing. Norman leaned back in his chair. He decided that those weren't clouds in the sky, or fog, or mist, or any other weather phenomenon. It was simply a blanket of static white, covering the town like a visual twin to the steady hum. What would it feel like to touch a sky like that? Would the white blanket feel like a cotton shroud, or like an electric fence?

"You know what, Pops? I wasn't planning on shooting that Collector when I ran upstairs. I was planning on getting shot, actually. And if the Collectors didn't shoot me, I was going to do the job myself."

Norman leaned toward Pops. "But when I smashed into that room, I stopped thinking and my hands took over. By the time I had a grip on myself, someone else was dead, and I, the murderous, suicidal idiot, was still alive. I couldn't even get myself killed properly. I couldn't even accomplish that much."

Pops stopped rocking, his eyes still unreadable behind his sunglasses. His familiar deep tan had disappeared, Norman noticed. The old man was as pale as anything now.

"You've got some steel inside you, Norman. That'll have to be enough." The old man pointed toward the swamp. "Go that way, son. Watch your step."

Norman stood up. "Thanks for the talk, Pops. You've been a good friend to me."

Norman held out his hand, but Pops didn't shake it.

"Sorry, son, but you don't want to touch me. I'd freeze your hand something awful."

Norman lowered his hand and started down the porch steps. The swamp hummed another notch louder, as if sensing his approach. Snakes hung from the cypress trees like coiled, glistening branches.

"Good luck, Norman."

Norman waved back to Pops. "I've come too far to fuck up now, haven't I?"

Pops frowned.

"I hope so, Norman. We all do."

Norman turned and headed into the swamp. He made it only a few steps into the hanging vines and mosquitoes before something strong lifted him from his feet and hauled him off into darkness.

29

He woke choking on a smell so bad he couldn't process it. No comparisons. No references. Just a stench so bad his eyes watered as badly as if he were weeping, and so he lay weeping in complete darkness, cold and uncomfortable. The pointed end of something dug into the middle of his back, and his legs were raised above his body, sending blood rushing to the back of his head. Also, the weight. So much weight pressing on his chest, making it hard to breathe.

And, oh God, he had fallen.

The bodies had dropped from above, knocked him off the cliff wall, and taken him for a ride. Now they pressed down on him, a massive weight of flesh and bone.

The walls of Norman's throat tightened and his stomach lurched, but he had nothing left to vomit. His stomach tried again anyway, and more tears streamed down his face. He tried moving his arms. Some give there, enough so he could push himself up on his elbows (the surface below him was flat and bony, probably a man's back). From there he tried to move his legs, but they were wedged solidly between two heavy spots. He kicked out, shoving as much energy into his legs as he could muster. He kept kicking until his heels broke free, then his calves, and then he was able to pull his knees under his body and push upward, heaving the bodies on top of him onto another part of the pile.

Norman took stock of himself in the dark. No major injuries, but his back hurt like hell and he was sticky, probably covered with blood and all other imaginable fluids. The grenade was still zipped inside his fleece's front pocket, but he'd lost the flashlight in the fall. Actually, he was glad for the dark right now, because he couldn't see what he was standing on.

But the humming.

The humming was intolerable.

Norman clenched his teeth and started climbing. He grabbed on to whatever was firm and didn't flop at his touch, and when he stuck his fingers into something wet and soggy, he tried not to imagine which part of a human's body it might be. Norman made it to the top of the pile and he stood up, each foot planted on top of someone's unmoving chest. He was more used to it now, but the stench was still horrible. Only a scavenger would find this sort of "food" palatable. Perhaps the Source was a huge vulture with sharp talons, its hooked nose eager to poke into eyes and ears, to sniff out the soft spots in a person's body and tear them away.

Norman felt the pile shifting and moved forward, hunched

over as he tried to keep his balance. He tripped over what might have been a woman's breast and caught himself by grabbing the clammy back of a bald man's head. He cursed and kept moving, not wanting to be buried alive, and after a lot of scrambling Norman made his way down to a floor that resembled rock. He shuffled carefully through the darkness, eyes aching for light as he stepped over bodies or, more frequently now, piles of bones. His eyes began playing little tricks on him, showing splotches of color floating against the darkness. The void hummed, maddening and shrill. Was it toying with him? Waiting for Norman to stumble around until he grew so severely dehydrated he passed out? Or was that light after all, in the distance?

Norman wiped his sticky palms on the front of his jeans until they felt reasonably clean. He started toward the light.

His starved eyes ached for definition, and the closer he got to the light, the more fossilized remains Norman could see piled all around him. Bones, bones, bones. So many bones.

Jordan.

Dad.

Mom.

Alice.

Eileen.

Helen.

Pops.

Cardenio.

Zero's parents.

Pastor Jake.

Maureen, and her murdered day-care children.

Seattle's Twenty Thousand.

And that was only a tiny sampling of the dead, the taken. A small slice of one country's deceased. What about India, what about China? What about Russia, Ireland, Germany, Spain, South Africa, Japan, Costa Rica, Turkey, Canada, Madagascar, Egypt, and Mexico? This was a veritable United Nations of death, a planet full of skeletal structures. Look at all this abandoned jewelry, all these tattered outfits and un-tied tennis shoes. Did enough trees exist to build so many coffins? How many bones did the human body have? Well, multiply that by nearly 6 billion and dump the whole heap at the bottom of the Grand Canyon. Or, better yet, the floor of the Atlantic Ocean. Then you'd get some idea of the scope, the absolute tremendous scope, of this hollow maze.

Norman halted at a bare spot on the ground and sat down. The cold had seeped through his layers of thermal clothing and sat throughout his body. His stomach ached, hungry despite the stench, and his mouth was so dry he no longer wanted whiskey, just a huge, cold glass of water. Maybe it would be a good idea to lie down for a while and take a nap. The bones weren't so uncomfortable when you found a smooth spot, an indentation in a pile. He could curl up and sleep and forget his hunger, his thirst, even the density grenade in his pocket.

Ah.

So, this was the Despair the whole world had been talking about.

Hell. If this was what Jordan had felt, no wonder she'd taken those pills. What a sweet, dreamy peace it promised. Norman took the grenade out and hefted it in his hand. He felt the weight of it, the reality of it, and remembered that it was too soon for him to lie down. He put the grenade back in his pocket, groggily returned to his feet, and continued in the direction of the light.

The haphazard maze of bones seemed to go on forever. Yet Norman did make steady progress, and the brighter the light grew, the louder the humming became, and as he turned the last corner, the Source appeared in front of him, so loud he covered his ears, and so luminous he had to shade his eyes.

Sometimes a man wakes in the middle of the night.

Sometime a man, even a blessed, happy man who loves his family and has felt only a vague twinge of depression his entire life, wakes in the middle of the night.

And sometimes that man slowly gets out of bed, careful not to wake his loving spouse, and slips on a bathrobe and shoes. He reaches into his nightstand, pulls out a gun, and goes downstairs. He leaves through the front door and, in his reverie, forgets to close it behind him. He goes on a late-night walk, perhaps through a forest, or a deserted city park, and at the end of the walk he sits down, places the gun's barrel in his mouth, and pulls the trigger. He does all that, and in the morning his family wakes to find the front door wide open and their home emptier. The man's family can spend the rest of their lives scouring their minds, memories, and medical records, but in the end they still won't totally comprehend what drove their loved one to kill himself, to leave them behind stumbling through a world that no longer makes much sense.

Norman knew about waking in the middle of the night and considering all your options. He also knew that sometimes, no matter how hard or far you searched, rational explanations for some occurrences simply couldn't be found. That was why the Source, and that he was about to die without any concrete answers regarding it, didn't surprise him.

He'd seen this sort of light before.

No dreamy ocean-floor environment this time. No patches of seaweed, sunken Spanish galleons, or drifting blue whales.

But the light.

The light was so beautiful.

Norman pulled the grenade from his pocket and stepped forward. The light remained where it was, allowing Norman to approach. It hummed so loudly, so radiantly, that Norman's mind sang with its song. He pulled the grenade's pin and sat down, setting the explosive gently on the ground in front of him. He unlaced his boots and took them off. He massaged his sore feet and pictured Zero walking back down the rails, returning to the sea. Pictured lovely, red-haired Maria, the scars on her wrists fading as she helped rebuild Seattle. He thought of his wife, how warm and right she'd once felt in his arms. He thought of home.

Epilogue

Zero followed the rails through the darkness. She tried not to think of the rats lining the tunnel walls, licking their oily whiskers as they waited for more soft dead humans. Could they see her in the dark? Smell her? That wouldn't be fair, not when she couldn't see anything at all. They'd be able to sneak up on her, bite her in the ankle, and trip her up. She'd fall. She'd land flat on her back and they'd jump on her, sinking their teeth into her cheeks while she screamed and punched and clawed. There'd be too many of them, and they'd be too used to the taste of people. She'd be eaten in five minutes flat, her bones licked clean by their sandpaper tongues.

Zero focused on the railroad beneath her feet, how it was leading her back to light. It was made of metal and wood. Good things. Strong things. The world was filled with strong things made out of wood and steel. She simply had to follow the rails, as Norman said. It didn't matter if she was eleven years old or thirty. Anyone could do this. Anyone.

Something brushed against her leg and Zero started to run. Almost immediately she tripped over one of the railroad ties and fell onto the rails. "Stay away!" she shouted into the dark as she jumped back to her feet. "Stay away, goddamn it." Nothing leaped for her throat, so she continued walking on trembling legs.

Behind her, the humming grew fainter. She wondered if this was because she was getting farther away from the void, or if it was because whatever lived in the void was now busy with Norman and no longer interested in her.

No. Better if she didn't think about that.

Hey.

Was that light up ahead?

Zero began walking faster, but the ground shook suddenly and the rails buckled, throwing the girl onto her back. A chunk of the tunnel's ceiling fell and smashed beside her head, covering her with rubble. Then, as abruptly as the tremors had begun, they stopped.

Zero lay still for a minute, wondering if there'd be more. She realized the small earthquake had been because of Norman.

He was gone.

He was gone, and the humming had stopped.

Zero stood up, ignoring the throbbing in her head as she stumbled forward. She could still see the tunnel's exit, but the ceiling had partially caved and chunks of rock were piled in the tunnel's mouth. When she reached the rubble, she found a small crack of light and crawled forward, squeezing through the debris and into daylight.

The railroad bridge was still intact. Down below, the Collectors' airport was deserted, the planes no longer taking off or landing. Norman's winter coat was thick, but the wind cut through it. The cold made Zero miss her father, the way he would warmly hug her off the ground, the way his face felt bristly against her cheek when he hadn't shaved for a few days. She missed her mom, too. She had dreamed of her parents while she was locked up on the ferry, and now she might be seeing them again. But still, she was scared. Was it wrong to want to keep living, to keep eating and laughing and growing older?

Zero crossed the bridge, keeping her body bent low against the crosswind. She made it to the other side, took a deep breath, and entered the second tunnel. She found more collapsed bits of tunnel here, but as before she was small enough to squeeze her way through. She took another food pill without missing a step and realized that her eyes had gotten accustomed to the darkness, had found a way to somehow discern *levels* of darkness, and she was able to walk the rails smoothly, without tripping, and the sound of the rats scuttling along the tunnel walls no longer bothered her much. Why would it? She'd been through the worst already, the worst possible things she could imagine. All her family was dead. All her friends were dead. She'd seen murder with her own eyes, seen a man rip open his own guts, and she'd been trapped for months on a fucked-up West Coast cruise liner. What did it matter if some stupid rat brushed against her ankle, tried to bite her? She'd deal with that when it came. She'd deal.

By the time Zero emerged from the second tunnel, she was so thirsty her throat had clamped shut (Death Island needed drinking fountains. Death Island needed a lot of amenities). She stepped into the gray daylight and ignored her swollen throat and quivering legs. No search helicopters swooped above the canyon, and she didn't care if they did. Maybe they'd bring her some water, some food that wasn't stuffed inside a pill. Whatever. Actually, she'd like to have a little talk with the Collectors. A little face-to-face. She'd be quick and her nails were long, as long as they'd ever been.

A few miles beyond the tunnel Zero collapsed and slept facedown on the rails. When she woke hours later, she realized that a train might have come along and crushed her, except they were no longer running, and that was because of Norman, too. She got up and kept walking, moving slower now, her breath labored and cracked as the canyon walls wavered around her like water, and she thought this might be what it felt like to be drunk, and then the distance began to waver like water, too, only that was because it was the ocean. The real ocean. She reached out, as if she could take it in her hands. She emerged from the mountains and the ground became sand. Gray, smooth sand, like an ashtray. She saw one ship, docked farther up the beach, and hundreds of Collectors lined single file along the shoreline, unmoving as they faced the ocean.

Zero stopped and rubbed her dry eyes. So many dark robes. What were they looking at, what did they see in the endless rise and fall of the waves? It was so cold and windy here. They must all be so cold. The Source was gone; it was time for all of them to go home.

She stomped across the sand. Her long, dark hair was wild and lashed against her face. She bit down on her tongue so the blood could grease it, and when she got within twenty feet of them, she shouted as loud as she could.

"Go home! Go home, go home, go home!"

The Collectors did not turn or acknowledge her in any way. She walked up and shouted again for them to go home. She grabbed a woman Collector by the collar and threw her to the sand. The woman regarded her with a blank, unfocused stare. She had gray eyes.

"I know you," Zero said. "You were in the van. You brought me to the ferry."

The woman's cheek twitched, but her gray eyes remained unfocused.

"You should go home now. You don't have to work for it anymore. It's over."

The woman stood up. She passed Zero as if the girl were invisible and rejoined the others in the line. Zero threw her hands up and walked away. Whatever. They could do what they wanted. Stare at the ocean forever, for all she cared.

The ship was farther than it appeared and the shifting beach was a bitch to walk on. Zero forced her legs up with each step, pulling them out of the sucking sand and setting them back down again. The sun had come out, but it hung too high in the sky and was too small, its light weak and watery (she could look at it without wincing, and she should not have been able to do that). How many miles until Kansas? She laughed at the idea of golden wheat fields and all that flat land, and as she laughed, she realized she was laughing like a crazy person, but that was okay for now as long as she kept moving and got away from them.

They were worse than crazy.

They were Long Gone.

She made it to the ship's dock. No railing, or anything like that. She might fall over the edge, her legs might give out and send her toppling into the frigid water, and the waves would come in and dash her against the shore and then suck her back out again, the undertow pulling her far out to sea, where she'd sink like a stone, her arms and legs limp at her sides, and then she'd settle on the ocean floor under a blanket of seaweed, and the fish would find her and nibble on her earlobes, they were soft and tasty to fish, and goddamn she needed to stop this before she really went crazy.

Zero bit her lower lip and stepped onto the dock. She'd come too far to fall off some stupid dock and drown in a couple feet of water. The dock swayed but she thought level thoughts. She focused her eyes ahead, on the ship. The ship, an old iron-ore freighter with a rusting belly, bobbed in the water. A metal ladder ran down its side and ended right above the dock, as if welcoming her. Zero would have bet anything that the ship's contents had already been unloaded and, deep down, the ship was glad to be rid of such rotten cargo, would welcome any efforts to cast off again and put as much water behind it and the island as possible.

Waves rolled past as Zero made her way to the end of the dock. She grasped the first chilled rung of the ship's ladder and began pulling herself up its side, suddenly not as tired as she thought. She climbed without pause and did not look down. She reached the top of the ladder and dipped forward over the ship's side. She swung one trembling leg over, then the other trembling leg, then she was standing on the ship's deck, the beach down below small from such a height.

The Collectors had started to move. They strode across the few remaining yards of beach in an unbroken line, cloaks whipping around their narrow bodies, and when they reached the water's edge, they simply kept walking. The tide splashed against their ankles, then their knees. Zero wrapped her arms around her chest and hugged herself. She couldn't make out individual faces, but they all kept staring straight ahead as they strode deeper and deeper into the surf. A big wave crashed and knocked many of them over, but the fallen got up again and kept going, and soon the dark, icy water came up to their chests, their bare necks. Zero moaned as the shortest people, the medium people, and then the tall people disappeared beneath the sea. More waves came up and crashed onto the beach, and it was as if they'd never been there, as if all those people who had once been clerks and accountants and firemen and dancers and bartenders had never existed at all. Only wind sweeping off the sea, the island floating on the ocean's surface like a piece of soot-covered trash.

Zero turned away and began exploring the ship. She found a bathroom. The bathroom sink's tap still worked, so she cupped her hands and drank. The water was icy cold and tasted like minerals. She drank until her throat stopped aching and her stomach was full, practically bursting, then she dried her hands on a paper towel and went back out to see what she could see.